A HEART TO KEEP

A HEART TO KEEP

Castles & Courtship
Series

ASHTYN NEWBOLD

CHAPTER ONE

A soft, eerie tune came from outside Emma Eastwood's window, which could mean only one thing.

Mr. Blyth was nearby.

He always whistled the same tune with no variation in its six notes, over and over again. Emma had never heard a more frightening sound, though she was grateful for it at the same time. It was a warning of sorts. It gave her time to hide.

She moved the drapes just enough to peer out the window. Mr. Blyth, with his stiff grey top hat and long, sweeping black tailcoat was walking up the front steps. His withered lips were puckered as he whistled his tune, and she could practically smell him through the glass. He was never without the unmistakable scent of beeswax and mildew. Spending all his hours in the ancient cathedral nearby had made him much like the structure—not only because of his scent. His skin had an undertone of grey like

1

the stone, and his tightly stretched cheeks over his angular face reminded her of a bare skull. He would fit in well with the centuries-old corpses that were buried in the church-yard and deep within the walls and floors of the cathedral.

Emma threw the drapes back over the window before lunging for her bed. She tossed back the covers and nestled herself underneath them. Her breath came quickly as she tugged at a few blonde strands of hair in her coiffure, making them stick out wildly so she would not be deemed presentable for Mr. Blyth. He had been calling upon her far too often of late, and despite her best efforts to deter him, she feared the worst.

A proposal would be coming soon.

She was running out of time.

She pulled the blankets up over her ears to drown out the sound of his whistling. It wouldn't be long before he was inside the drawing room waiting for her. After that, Tom, Emma's stepbrother, or Arabella—his wife, would be coming up the stairs to inform Emma of her visitor.

If she pretended to be unwell, she might not be forced to have her hair fixed in order to go have an uncomfortable conversation with Mr. Blyth about the impending destruc-tion of all the wicked men that Emma might meet if she ever ventured outside of their small coastal town in West Sussex. He liked to try to use his authority in the parish to convince her that he was the only high-minded, principled man she might ever meet. He would be dismayed to know that when he spoke such words, he actually made her think the oppo-site of him. And although she didn't know *many* high-minded, principled men, she did know one man who was much better than Mr. Blyth.

Unfortunately, she hadn't seen *that man* for two years, yet she was forced to see Mr. Blyth almost daily.

Just as she predicted, a knock sounded on her door.

"Yes?" she said in a groggy voice. She kept her eyes half-closed to add credibility to her act.

The door opened and Arabella came into view through Emma's squinted eyelids. Her long, slender neck was covered in jewels, her dark hair perfectly arranged in a chignon with loose curls around her face. She was accomplished at many things—French, Italian, drawing, playing the pianoforte—and making Emma feel as unwelcome as possible.

"What on earth are you doing in bed?" Arabella hissed. She marched forward and threw the blankets off Emma. A chill ran over her skin as her body heat escaped. "Mr. Blyth is here to see you."

Emma blinked up at Arabella, genuine terror seizing her limbs. She couldn't face Mr. Blyth, not when she was so close to escaping him. She had a plan, one that she hadn't yet told Arabella, and especially not Tom. "I don't feel well." Emma sat up partially, making the movement as slow and weak as possible.

"You don't look well either." Arabella's face crumpled in disgust. "What has happened to your hair?" She gave a frustrated sigh. Emma's stomach sank as she recognized the unrelenting glint in Arabella's eyes. "I am going to call for the maid to repair the monstrosity and then you can go greet Mr. Blyth. He might be minded to propose to you today."

That was precisely why she couldn't see him. "I am truly quite faint. I should stay in bed."

Arabella's nostrils flared, and then she leaned forward until her face was close to Emma's. "If this is some sort of trick to avoid an engagement to Mr. Blyth, then you are a fool. I already told you the agreement Tom and I have come to, did I not? You are aware of what will happen if you do not marry Mr. Blyth?" Her threats rang in Emma's ears.

Emma nodded, swallowing hard. "I am acutely aware."

Arabella's spine straightened, and her expression smoothed over. "Good. You would do well not to forget."

Emma lowered her head down to her pillow and held Arabella's gaze as she backed away from her bedside. Of course she hadn't forgotten. How could she forget how it felt to be so unwanted? In Arabella's eyes, and even Tom's, Emma was a pest. She lived in the dark corners of the house, uninvited to parties, never introduced to guests, tucked away in her room where no one could see her. She was the stepsister Tom had never asked for when his father married Emma's mother. And then she became the ward he had never asked for when both of them died.

Tom's father had died of a fever first, and so Emma's mother had taken care of Tom. That was why he felt responsible for Emma after her mother fell ill of a similar ailment years later. It was only guilt that made Tom agree to be Emma's guardian at all. After Tom married Arabella the year before, everything changed. Suddenly Tom's sense of responsibility faded along with his compassion. Arabella wanted Emma gone, and so Tom did too. He seemed to have forgotten his promise to Emma's mother.

In the younger years of her life, Mama had been a prima donna in London, singing on the biggest stages in all of England. She had caught the attention of Emma's father, who was an untitled but successful gentleman. Despite all the prattle of his family concerning the reputation and social ranking of prima donnas, he had still married her. Such fates were not often obtained by professional women, but Mama had always given Emma the choice to pursue such a dream if she longed for it, even if it meant she would be subject to criticism and attacks on the morale of her character for choosing such a path. That was something Emma had always admired about her mother. She had chosen to use her own wings, and she had never tried to clip her daughter's.

Emma's father had died long ago, shortly after Emma's birth, and the estate was, quite unfortunately, entailed. Mama had chosen to marry again rather than return to sing in London for the sake of giving Emma a better upbringing. There had been nothing wrong with Emma's stepfather, nor his son Thomas.

Until Tom married Arabella.

After a few months, Tom and Arabella let Emma out of hiding, but with one condition: she was not allowed to sing. The first time Arabella had heard her voice, she had told her she sounded like a toad and that she was never allowed to sing again within the walls of that house, and especially not around guests. Emma knew she didn't sound like a toad, because she had a voice like her mother, who had trained her from the time she was a child. *"This voice will catch you a great deal of attention one day, Emma,"* she had cautioned. *"It is up to you to choose how you use it."*

It was that *attention* that Arabella didn't want Emma to have. If any attention was to be had in that house, it belonged solely to Arabella and her talents.

They had introduced Emma to the few acquaintances they had in the small seaside town, one of whom was Mr. Blyth, who was regrettably the only eligible bachelor in town. Tom and Arabella didn't care that he smelled of beeswax and mildew and resembled a corpse. All they cared about was the fact that he could take Emma, the burden that she was, away from them for good.

Emma had been obvious about her aversion to the idea, yet she had spent many weeks accepting his calls because of Arabella's threats. Emma hadn't entirely believed that Tom would send her away to fend for herself, but the agreement Arabella had made with him could not be denied. Emma had two options: Accept the proposal of Mr. Blyth, the only eligible gentleman in town, or be banished from their house to make her own way. In most instances, that meant Emma would have to somehow find work as a governess or maid or any similar profession. She would have to give up any status she had inherited from her father's position as a gentleman. Arabella had thought that decision would be easy for Emma, but marrying Mr. Blyth was *not* an option.

Emma had a much better one that Arabella hadn't considered.

She could audition to sing in London.

If her mother had done it, so could she. It had never been Emma's dream, and she knew what scrutiny she would face, but with marriage to Mr. Blyth as the alternative, she saw no other way.

She had been waiting for the right moment to tell her stepbrother and his wife about her plan to leave, but it hadn't come. She had decided that the best option would be to slip away unnoticed, leaving behind a letter explaining her departure.

"I hope you feel well soon," Arabella said, snapping Emma out of her thoughts. Her voice dripped with vexation. "*Only* so you can accept calls from Mr. Blyth again. He is your only offer, Emma. If you do not marry him, you shall never marry at all and you will no longer live under Tom's protection or that of any other man." Her eyes darkened. "Keep that in mind."

Emma didn't respond, holding Arabella's gaze with as much ferocity as she could. When Arabella had first married Tom, Emma had found it difficult not to shrink with Arabella's attempts at dominating a conversation. But over time, Emma had learned to hold her own. It was better not to respond. It was obvious how greatly it vexed Arabella when Emma remained collected and silent. She seemed to crave uproar and a reaction to her belittling remarks, so Emma had vowed never to give her what she sought.

With a huffed breath, Arabella turned on her heel and marched out of the room, throwing the door shut firmly behind her.

After waiting a few seconds, Emma slunk to the floor and reached under her bed to withdraw her traveling valise. She ought to start packing. It would be better to leave *before* Mr. Blyth offered a proposal, not after having to reject him.

She opened the valise, withdrawing her reticule. Inside were all the meager funds she had gathered over the last several months. Tom provided her with a minuscule amount of pin money, but without spending a penny, she had managed to scrape up enough to provide her with transport to London and hopefully the first month or two of lodging while she was there. With any luck, she would be employed and earning her own way before that money ran out.

Her heart pounded as she kneeled on the floor and filled the valise with her few most valuable items. Her finest dresses, her mother's necklace...and all of her letters from her friend Harry.

Upon seeing his writing, her heart pinched deep inside her chest. Two years was a very long time. How much had he changed since she had last seen him? She had accepted that she would never know the answer. A lifetime without him would feel very long if she didn't learn to forget him.

She paused as she picked up his latest letter, rereading a portion of it. It was her least favorite letter of his. She wondered why she kept it at all, but she had decided that it was a good reminder of her path in life. She could no longer hold onto old hopes; she needed to move forward, and this letter reminded her of that fact. There were times when hope simply needed to be crushed and killed swiftly in order to make way for new dreams. That was what this letter did for her, and so she read it for the hundredth time.

Dear Emma,

How has it been nearly two years since I've seen you? I suppose I took for granted the many summers we spent at Stansham. I find it rather strange that so much has changed in both our lives. I do hope that our paths may cross again one day. Since inheriting Garsley Castle, I have been busier than I ever thought possible. There is so much potential in this grand structure, and I have many ideas that are too elaborate to write in this letter. I hope you will visit the castle someday, and I hope you know you are welcome any time. How is life for you? You mentioned that your stepbrother married, so I must offer my congratulations. In similar news, I am also to be married. You are likely collapsing in shock at that notion, and I confess I am quite surprised as well. The wedding won't take place until my betrothed returns from her trip to the Cotswolds.

Emma stopped reading, taking a deep breath as she set the letter gingerly inside her valise. She had an entire stack of letters from Harry that she had collected over the years, and she treasured those ones—the ones he had written before his heart had been claimed by his betrothed.

Her chest ached as she continued arranging her belongings inside the valise. Why had she reread the letter? Each time she did, it hurt a little more. Was she hoping that somehow the words would change with each reading? They were inked on the page, and they might as well have been etched in stone. Harry would never lie about something like marriage. As much as she wished it was a lie, she knew better.

Mr. Blyth truly was her only option, and she would rather never marry at all. It wouldn't have mattered if he had been even a dashing earl instead of a decaying clergyman. Harry was the only one she had ever wanted. The first summer she had met him at Stansham, the estate in Cornwall that belonged to a mutual friend of both Harry and Emma's parents, she had only been twelve years old. He had been fourteen. Year after year, she admired Harry more, until her admiration had reached its capacity. By the time she was twenty-one, the last time she had visited, she had realized what happens to admiration when it overflows. It becomes love.

Now, at twenty-three, she was still pathetically in love with Harry. And he was in love with someone else.

She wanted to be happy for him, but the effort was painful. If she never saw him again, she might be able to forget him instead. Keeping his letters wouldn't help her accomplish that goal, but she wasn't quite ready to let go. She wouldn't be seeing him at Stansham ever again, not since Joseph, the owner of the estate, had died the year before and the house had been passed to his nearest relative.

She had passed Garsley Castle once on horseback since learning of Harry's inheritance, but she had never stopped to visit. When he had first inherited it, he had left for London shortly after, so she hadn't found a reason to tour it if he wasn't even there. It was fifteen miles from where Emma currently lived, settled among large, ancient trees and a moat. The location was perfect. It faced the distant sea, with what she imagined would be a perfect view of the pebble beach and sunset.

Her journey to London would put all of her feelings for Harry behind her. It was a new beginning, one that both frightened and excited her. Mama would have supported her decision not to marry Mr. Blyth, even if Arabella and Tom would call her a fool. That one thought was what comforted her as she sat at her desk and wrote her farewell letter to Tom. Arabella would know about the letter, but she didn't deserve one of her own.

· · ·

Tom,

Since you have made your wishes clear, I have decided to leave your home in my own way rather than allowing myself to be forced into a marriage that you know I never wanted. Send my regrets to Mr. Blyth. I doubt you will worry for me, but if by chance you do, know that I am on my way to London. If you ever wish to see me again, you may come watch me sing on the largest of stages there as my mother once did.

She hesitated, holding her quill above the page for a few seconds before adding,

Thank you for looking after me all these years.
    Sincerely,
    Emma

CHAPTER TWO

With quiet footsteps, Emma moved toward the salver in the entryway and placed her letter atop it. The house was quiet and dark, and the sun had yet to rise fully in the sky. She picked up her valise, unexpected tears stinging her eyes as she took one more glance around the house. She had spent years there. It was the last place she had seen her mother alive and well, flitting through the house with dignity and purpose and a constant smile on her face. It was tragic how quickly circumstances could change. Emma had never imagined her mother's brightness would succumb to a simple fever, nor had she ever imagined that she would be fleeing off to London on her own.

Yet here she was. She took a deep breath, turning her back to all the memories that lived within those walls. She could keep the good ones in her heart, and the rest she could leave far behind.

Before the servants could take their stations and witness

her departure, she slipped out the front door and across the neatly trimmed lawn. Her valise was heavy as she made the long walk into the nearby town, but she managed the weight by switching it from one hand to the other frequently. She wore the reticule on her wrist, the one with all her money where she could easily access it when it came time to pay the coachman. The footpath that led to town was one she had taken many times, but the three mile walk was usually more bearable than it was that day. The weight of her valise added to the exertion, and soon her forehead was damp with perspiration. As the sun began to rise and the heat came into effect, she tugged her bonnet down farther, keeping as much shade as possible. At least she could rely on the spring breeze to keep her cool.

By the time she reached town, she took a short rest, setting her valise down beside her as she sat against the cool stone of a building. Catching her breath, she glanced around at the nearby shops. She had never ventured out so early before, so she was surprised to see how forlorn the street was. Not a soul was in sight, though she could hear movement inside the nearby bakery. The other shops and costermongers had yet to open business for the day.

She had come earlier than was necessary, but she wanted to escape before Tom and Arabella awoke. It would be an hour before the coachman came to convey her to London, but at least she was safely away from home for the time being.

Her stomach grumbled, and her mouth watered at the scents coming from the bakery. Before continuing her journey, she would have to buy a pastry or two.

She pressed a hand to her pestering stomach and closed

her eyes, trying to focus on images of soft buns and the flaky, buttery crusts of her favorite tartlets and pies rather than the nervousness gnawing at her insides. Dwelling on the hunger rather than the fear was much more bearable. Despite her efforts, the worry still crept back in. What if she failed her audition? What if her voice was as dreadful as Arabella told her it was? As much as she had tried to maintain her confidence, the constant blows from Arabella had done a bit of damage. Was there any truth to Arabella's words? Not only had she attacked Emma's singing, but she had also told her how plain she was—how she might never find an offer of marriage even if Tom did afford her a Season and opportunity to meet men outside of their small part of West Sussex. Was she pretty enough to perform in London? Would her talent be enough?

A tight knot of dread spread through her stomach, replacing the hunger altogether. The pastries no longer sounded appetizing. She felt quite ill, in fact. She drew a deep breath, and then another, keeping her eyes closed. All would be well. She needed to believe in herself as her mother had, but that was difficult when her mother was no longer there.

She bit back the emotion in her throat, keeping her eyelids down to prevent her tears from escaping. *Don't you dare be a watering pot, Emma,* she scolded herself. Her journey had barely begun. She couldn't be crying already.

Her skin prickled with awareness, and she opened her eyes to see a man standing just a few feet in front of her. Her muscles tensed, her heart picking up speed. His clothing was tattered at the knees, the hem of his dirty white shirt unraveled. His face and hair were dusted with dirt, and his wild green eyes were fixed on her valise. She frantically glanced in all directions, but there was no one on the street besides this man and Emma. When had he snuck up on her? Why had she been daft enough to close her eyes?

"Good mornin, miss," the man said. His voice was worse than Mr. Blyth's. It sent a shiver over her spine. His teeth were stained yellow and two of the front ones were missing.

"Good morning," she muttered with a quick smile. Her heart pounded faster. Instinctively, she tightened her grip on both her valise and reticule and made to stand. She was cornered against the wall of the building, but if she could slip to one side or the other she might be able to make it to the bakery door in the hopes that the baker inside would see her and let her in.

Before she was fully to her feet, the man lunged forward. Emma shrieked, swinging her elbow in his direction. It struck him in the ribs, but it hardly affected his pursuit. He took hold of her reticule first. "Help!" she shouted, kicking his leg as hard as she could. He grunted, his face twisting in anger as he tugged harder on the reticule. She resisted, crying out in pain as the ribbon dug into her wrist, the friction rubbing her skin raw. The man tugged hard enough to break the ribbon.

"Give that back!" she yelled, surprised at the anger in her own voice as she grasped for it. Desperation rose inside her. She needed that money.

Instead of obeying her demands, the man wrenched the valise from her other hand, taking off running across the street and down an alley.

No. No, no, no. She frantically chased after him across the cobblestones. What would she do if she found him? She was powerless to take her belongings back. He had stolen them so easily—she hadn't even had a chance. Her wrist throbbed with pain and tears welled in her eyes. By the time she reached the entrance of the alley, he was already gone.

All her money—her passage to London—was gone with him. Not only that, but so was all her finest clothing, her mother's necklace, and Harry's letters. All of them. Tears cascaded down her cheeks as she leaned her back against the inside wall of the alley. She put her face in her hands, her body shaking with a quiet sob. She kicked at the edge of a cobblestone in frustration. What was she to do?

Across the street, the bakery door opened, the stout baker with his bald, glistening head holding open the door for his first customer.

Now she couldn't even buy a pastry.

Her tears came anew, and she hid herself in the shadows of the alley for several minutes and let them fall. If she returned home, it would take months to replenish the money she had saved, and by then, she would be forced to marry Mr. Blyth. Arabella's patience was too thin to allow Emma the chance to save her money again and leave for London. Tom had always been ashamed of his stepmother's past as a prima donna, so he would never willingly pay Emma's way to go audition in London. The only outcome Emma could see now was a future with Mr. Blyth.

Her stomach lurched with terror. She had been so close to an escape, and all in an instant, her circumstances had altered permanently. She had no money. There would be no London. No audition. No hope for a future of her own. It was starvation and living on that very street, or a dignified return home to accept Mr. Blyth's proposal.

She drew a shaky breath, weighing out her options in her mind. Even if there were somewhere else for her to go, she didn't have a single penny to pay a coachman. She couldn't even afford to ride on a mail coach. All she had was the clothing on her back and her own legs to carry her. She hadn't even worn any jewelry that she might sell, and all that she owned of value had been inside that valise.

She wiped at her cheeks as she thought of Harry's letters inside of it. It was fitting that she would lose them just as quickly as she had lost him. Did it even matter? Why should she keep them for so long when he had likely disposed of her letters long ago? Of all the items she had lost inside her valise and reticule, those letters from Harry were the least valuable. All they did was haunt her, so at least that was one good thing that had come of the robbery. Someone *had to* take those letters from her, or she would read them over and over until the day she died. It was better this way.

Her brow contracted as the last of her tears dried. At the end of the one letter she had read the day before, the one in which Harry had informed her of his engagement—he had reaffirmed his invitation for her to visit him at Garsley Castle. Even after becoming engaged, he had still invited her. She had vowed to herself that she wouldn't go, but now...

Her heart picked up speed as an idea formed in the back of her mind. Could she go to Garsley? It would be temporary, of course, but it might give her time to think. Harry might know people in his circle of acquaintances who could connect her with a family in need of a governess or other household staff. There was even the possibility that he was planning a visit to London in the near future, a journey that she could ask to accompany him on.

Could she do it? Her heart protested the idea of seeing Harry—of being near him while knowing he was engaged. It would be torturous, yes, but so would being married to Mr. Blyth. She knew her place—she knew she and Harry couldn't be together, so as long as she remembered that, it would be harmless. Surely the visit would do something to change her fate. If Harry knew the future she faced, he would do what he could to help her. It was in his nature to be kind. He always had been. Though she had vowed to herself that she wouldn't risk the pain of seeing him again, she could now think of no other option.

Her mind raced as she considered the idea from every angle. It was a long walk to the castle, especially now that she had come into town. From home, Garsley was fifteen miles away. From where she currently was in town, it would be eighteen, and she had already walked three miles that morning. It was madness, but the idea refused to leave her head. Without food or water, it would be a challenge, but she knew she could do it if she set her mind to it.

She considered sneaking back into Tom's house on her way to gather some food and water, but decided against it. He might try to stop her. She could endure for a few long hours of walking. Whether she could endure the heartbreak of seeing Harry again was another question entirely.

Sniffing away the last of her tears, she stepped out of the alleyway empty-handed. She tried to think of something positive, but all she could come up with was that she didn't have to carry that heavy valise for eighteen miles. The thought did little to lift her spirits.

Her throat was already dry, and her stomach gave yet another rumble. Her wrist still hurt from that wicked thief tugging on her reticule, so she examined the damage. It was red and slightly swollen, the beginning of a bruise already forming on one side. She could hardly believe she was about to embark on such a journey on foot, but she couldn't bear the thought of the alternative. She had written in that letter to Tom that she was leaving, and so she had to leave. She was not a liar. She couldn't return home in defeat. It would completely ruin her grand departure.

The fully risen sun beat down on her as she began her walk. She was grateful for her bonnet and the lingering breeze. She walked as quickly as she could, veering slightly off course to the shade of a tree to take a break every few miles. Her legs ached each time she stood and resumed her journey. She was not accustomed to walks like this. The most she had ever walked in one day was six miles—into town and back again. Any genteel young lady would find her completely mad for taking on such a feat, but she was determined.

Her resting periods became longer as the day went on. She had passed the castle once before, and she was certain she remembered the way. Her memory was remarkable when it came to facts about Harry.

When she was approximately halfway there, she stopped on a particularly soft patch of grass and stretched out, letting her eyelids drift closed as she lay on the grass. She hadn't slept the night before in anticipation of her escape, and now her lack of sleep was catching up to her. The thought of walking twice what she already had nearly brought more tears to her eyes. Perhaps with a short nap, she could return refreshed.

Her whirlwind of thoughts faded as she drifted off to sleep.

Emma awoke to a pang of hunger in her stomach. She struggled to swallow against her dry throat. As her eyes opened, they settled on the peach-streaked sky. She sat upright in an instant, rubbing the sleep from her eyes. "*Drat. Drat, drat, drat.*" She scrambled to her feet, groaning with the ache in her muscles. How long had she slept? It must have been hours. She still had hours of walking ahead of her, several of which she would have to do in complete darkness. She scolded herself repeatedly as she limped off toward the footpath. Walking through woods in the dark was not wise, espccially not alone, but she no longer had a choice. Her sleep had given her new energy, but it wasn't worth the cost.

The sun quickly fell below the horizon, and without the heat of the day, she managed to move a little faster. Even so, the half-moon did little to illuminate her path. Every sound in the woods around her made her jump. She could already imagine Harry's reaction when she told him how far she had walked to reach him. She could envision his wide brown eyes blanketed in dark lashes, the gaping look of disbelief on his face.

She had no way of tracking the time, but the sun had been down for at least two hours by her estimation by the time she cleared the woods and came to the base of a grassy hill. She recognized it. She had only a few more miles to go. A whimper escaped her chest as she carried her tired legs up the steep incline. She slipped once on a patch of mud, landing on her knees. She gritted her teeth as she pushed herself up on her sore wrist and found her footing again. By the time she reached the castle, she would be far too late to go knocking on the doors. Presenting herself so muddy and tattered was inevitable, but she might have to wait until morning.

Emma's eyes had adjusted well to the darkness, and by the time the castle came into view, she could see it clearly in the starlight. The wind from the nearby sea whipped at Emma's muddy skirts, and she could hear the water rolling up on the shore, even from the distance. The sea was just an unending expanse of darkness topped with stars, but she remembered how breathtaking the view was from her location. She could only imagine how much better it was from inside the castle through the clear glass of the windows.

Every part of her body ached as she made her way toward the dark mass of stone. At one point in history, the arched entry to the property near the gatehouse would have been heavily guarded, but now, it was empty and quiet as she dragged herself the remaining steps across the bridge to the castle grounds. The moat was unmoving, a sheet of black glass. Her heart was already thudding with regret over her choice. She had been invited to visit, yes, but surely not like this. Now that Harry was engaged, did his invitation truly still stand, or was it a formality? His betrothed wouldn't like the idea of a young lady so close to Harry, even if she was only his friend. She blamed her indecisive thoughts on her lack of food and water. The faintness in her head and unease in her stomach were growing worse with each step. She had to stop to rest her head in her hands as she nearly fainted.

Taking a deep breath, she examined her surroundings. None of the castle windows were lit, which told Emma that it was far too late to go knocking on the front doors. Her timidity battled her sense. Though she was hungry and thirsty, her pride demanded that she wait until morning to ask for entrance into the main part of the castle, even if she had to sleep outside on the grass. In one of his letters, Harry had told her that he and his mother, as well as their staff, lived in various parts of the domestic buildings within the castle along the curtain walls. He had described the great hall as one of the grandest he had ever seen. So many other parts of the castle were, it seemed, unoccupied.

The keep towered high near the gatehouse, and to her surprise, the door hung open, swaying with the wind. Had it blown open by accident? Was the lock in disrepair? She crept toward it, peering inside. A tall stone staircase was to the immediate right of the doorway.

She hesitated.

Before she could lose her nerve, she stepped inside.

Her head ached as she climbed the steep stone staircase. The first floor was in disrepair, the stone floors and walls chipped and worn. A shiver ran over her as she thought of all that might have taken place in that castle in the centuries since it had been built. It was amazing that it was still standing at all. Had only parts of the castle been restored? Surely Harry and his mother weren't living in a stone chamber such as this. It was spacious inside, but there were no furnishings. She hadn't really expected to find a bed, but she had hoped for at least a chair or settee of some sort.

There were still at least three more floors, but she was too weak and tired to scale so many more stairs. Instead, she lay down on the floor and nestled her head into the crook of her arm. That would have to suffice as her pillow for the night. As weary as she was, it wouldn't be difficult to sleep, even on the hard floor. Her nerves spiraled through her stomach as she thought of the next morning when she would have to explain herself to Harry. At present, she was trespassing on his property without his knowledge. Perhaps she could leave that part out.

In the dark of the castle keep, Emma sang a quiet melody, enjoying the way the sound echoed in the vast space. She might not have been at her final destination, but at least she was now free to sing as much as she wished.

CHAPTER THREE

Harry Coleman strode across the grass, paper and board in hand as he made his way to the future hotel of Garsley Castle.

If he were to fulfill his dream of having it in operation within two years, he would need to make orders for the furnishings as soon as possible. He couldn't make a final decision without Miss Fitzroy, his betrothed, but it was becoming one of his favorite pastimes to simply stand in the space and envision what it could become. New ideas were born each time he set foot inside, and he suspected today would be no different. The sun had only just risen for the day, but he hated wasting time. If he was to be a successful businessman, he couldn't be sleeping while others were awake, working and dreaming.

He paused at the open door of the keep, examining the broken lock. His brow furrowed. That was a new problem. The lock had been extremely rusted the last time he had checked, but now it was completely broken through. The nearby sea was unforgiving with its winds at times, so he would have to fortify the locks with new metal. He scribbled that down on his paper before tucking the pencil behind his ear and walking through the door.

As he had done dozens of times, he made his way cheerfully up the staircase. His legs had grown accustomed to the steep climb, so there was nothing to make him pause on his ascent. Just as the thought crossed his mind, a soft voice floated down the staircase, a song he had heard before.

He stopped abruptly.

His heart leaped, and he stood perfectly still, one foot on the step above.

Someone was on the first floor...and she was singing. He listened to the soft, angelic voice for several seconds, his heart in his throat. Had he lost his mind? Surely he was imagining all of it.

But what if he wasn't?

The voice was just like one he had heard many times, summer after summer, at Stansham. He had never heard a voice equal to it in perfect pitch, vibrato, and tone. It was captivating in every way, and he would have recognized it anywhere.

He took one more careful step up the staircase. Even if it *was* Emma's voice, why on earth would she be there inside the keep just after dawn? It didn't make sense, yet he couldn't deny the familiarity of the sound. Was it some other lady who had broken the lock and sneaked inside the keep for shelter? Did she just happen to sound like Emma? Harry knew his questions would be answered as soon as he reached the top of the stairs, but his mind and heart still raced as he ascended the final few steps.

He came around the corner, taking in the stony walls and floor of the open space and a few arched doorways leading to the rooms. He blinked, clearing his vision to ensure that his eyes weren't deceiving him. Emma Eastwood was standing near the window that faced the sea, finishing the ends of a braid in her hair as she sang her quiet melody. Her profile faced him, so she hadn't yet noticed his presence there.

"Emma?" he choked.

She whirled to face him, jumping back a pace. The long golden hair she had just been braiding came unraveled at the end. The front of her skirts were caked in mud, and her eyes were surrounded with dark circles, the rest of her skin pale. "Harry!" She took a step forward, then backward, as if she didn't know exactly where to go. "I am so very sorry. Please allow me to explain." She wrung her hands together nervously and then winced, examining her wrist.

Harry gathered his wits and walked forward, concern flooding through him. "What—what happened to you? What are you doing here?" He leaned down to look at her face, noting the puffiness of her eyelids and the smears of dirt on her cheeks. Her blue eyes, wide and innocent as always, stared up at him. Though he hadn't seen her in two years, and he had *never* seen her so disheveled, her eyes were still exactly the same. A surge of fond memories came with them, and he could hardly look away.

"I didn't mean for you to find me like this." She sighed. "I-I hoped to come to your front door in a respectable manner later this morning. What are *you* doing here? It's barely past dawn."

Harry laughed in his throat. "I own this castle. I think

my presence in the keep is less alarming than yours." His gaze flitted over her face. He was overcome by the waves of relief that came at seeing her again, and the shock he felt was immeasurable.

"That is true." She groaned as she put a hand to her forehead. The front of her wrist was bruised and red.

She began lowering it, but Harry reached for it before she could hide it from view. He turned her hand over to examine the damage to her wrist. She held still, staring up at him as he brought the wound close to his face to inspect if further. The skin was raw, a bruise surrounding the ring of red that circled her wrist. His concern only intensified. "How did this happen?" he asked. If someone had hurt her, he would have their head.

She looked down at the stone floor, taking a shaky breath. "Shall I start from the beginning?"

He took in her ragged appearance. Had she slept on the stone floor? How long had she been there? Her half-lidded eyes and slouched posture made him even more concerned. He began shaking his head. "Not yet. You need food and water and...a bath." He gave a wry smile at the mortification in her features.

He hadn't realized that he still held her hand. She slipped it slowly away from his grasp. "If it isn't too much trouble, that does sound very nice. But I—I don't have any other clothing." A resounding rumble came from somewhere inside her stomach. She looked up bashfully. "I didn't have anything to eat or drink yesterday."

Harry couldn't imagine what she might have been through, or *why*, but he was desperate to help her. He could ask for an explanation later, but at the moment, her well-being was more important. "I will see if you can borrow something from my mother to wear. With a few alterations, it might suffice for now."

Emma's eyes were halfway closed, her brow contracted as she took as step toward the staircase. "I don't feel well." She blinked hard and reached for his arm.

He steadied her, but she continued to mumble with her eyes closed. "I walked eighteen miles."

Eighteen? Why the devil had she walked so far?

She limped along beside him until they reached the stairs. There was no way she was going to make it down in her current state, nor should she try. "I'll have to carry you."

Her eyes opened a little wider, that same hint of reservation reflected in them. "Oh, no, there is no need for that." Her throat bobbed with a labored swallow as she lowered her foot down the first step. She grimaced, but quickly turned it into a smile. Her balance faltered, and Harry grabbed her upper arm to stop her from toppling over.

"I'm afraid there *is* a need for it," he said. Before she could protest again, he wrapped one arm around her upper back and the other beneath her knees, lifting her off the floor.

"Please don't fall," she whimpered, closing her eyes.

"You think I'm going to fall?" Harry scoffed. "You nearly fainted and fell on your head on the stone stairs."

A faint smile touched her lips, which was a relief. He scowled as he studied her face and all the dirt and dark circles around her eyes. If she had wanted to visit him, why had she come so far on foot? There must have been some other reason for her journey. He walked as quickly as he could down the stairs and across the courtyard to the entrance of the furnished area of Garsley.

Fortunately most of his staff was awake and working, so he managed to find a maid to follow him to one of the guest rooms. He set Emma down on the bed, leaving her to the maid, Isabel's, care before going to the kitchen to gather up bread, fruit, ham, and a glass and pitcher of water. By the time he returned to her room, Isabel had already fetched a bowl of hot water and was wiping the dirt from Emma's face with a cloth.

Emma's eyes flickered in Harry's direction, following each of his movements as he pulled a chair close to her bedside and set the tray of food beside her.

"Thank you," she muttered, her eyes still fixed on him.

A slow smile curled Harry's lips. "What are you staring at?"

"You." She pursed her lips. "You look like...well, you look like you *own a castle.*"

"Do I?" Harry chuckled. "How so?"

She shrugged, reaching for the glass of water first. He waited patiently as she drank the whole thing, then he poured her another, which she finished just as quickly. She then picked up the bread, eating it with impressive speed. Between bites, she said, "you command the room. You look quite grown up."

"Did I not before? I am only two years older than the last time you saw me, and I was quite grown up even then."

"I don't know how to explain it," she said, her eyes wrinkling at the corners. Her expression settled into one of quiet curiosity. "Perhaps it's because you are to be married."

His breath caught in his lungs, and he cleared his throat. "Yes, I am." He had never liked talking to Emma about marriage and their individual futures. In all the summers they had spent in one another's company, they had rarely spoken of it. He could still remember one summer at Stansham when she had mentioned a young man who lived nearby in Cornwall, one who she found endearing. The fact that Harry still remembered his name—August Moon—was unsettling. Similarly, if Harry had ever brought up the subject of any young lady of interest, their conversation had become...awkward.

"Who is the lady and how did you meet her?" Emma asked in a hesitant voice. "Your letter was very vague on the subject." She paused, her eyes widening slightly. "Or are you already married? I suppose you didn't mention when she would be returning from her trip."

"No, we are not married yet." He swallowed. "But I cannot tell you all of this until you explain to me why you broke into my keep." He cast her a pointed look—one that was soft enough to convey his forgiveness of the intrusion, strange as it was.

"I didn't break in." She finished her bread and moved on to the grapes, popping two in her mouth at once. She took a long time to chew before swallowing and raising a hand in defense. "The lock on the door was already broken and the door was open. I arrived too late to disturb you, so I decided to rest for the night inside. I didn't think you would find me at dawn. I'm very sorry."

"I heard you singing the moment I stepped inside." Harry smiled. "Even when you are tired and hungry, your voice is beautiful."

She stared at him for a moment before tearing her gaze away. "Thank you."

Why did she seem surprised to hear that? He studied her scrunched brow as she finished the last of her food. She took a deep breath, her gaze flickering around the room rather than meeting Harry's. "Coming here was not part of my original plan. As you know, I was under the care of my stepbrother. After he married...well, his wife was not fond of me and my presence in her household. She continued to invite the one eligible gentleman in town, Mr. Blyth, to call upon me and court me. I am not fond of him." She gulped. "Arabella—Tom's wife—gave me no choice but to wed Mr. Blyth or be sent out of the house for good. I saved as much money as I could to make my escape to London to audition to be a prima donna there." She glanced at Harry's face, as if checking for his reaction. "While I was waiting in town for the coachman, I was robbed. My valise and my reticule were stolen and I could think of nowhere else to go but here." She blinked, a sheen of moisture in her eyes.

Harry's mind reeled as he comprehended the tale. If he had known Emma was in such dire straits, he would have done all he could to help her *before* she had chosen to walk so far alone. How could anyone treat Emma so cruelly? To have her in her stepbrother's household could not have been burdensome at all. She was a delight to be around. She was thoughtful and caring and kind. She didn't deserve to be given such a harsh ultimatum. "And your wrist?"

"It was hurt when the thief pulled at my reticule." Her jaw tensed.

Harry's chest tightened with anger.

"I promise I do not plan to stay for long," she said, "but I hoped that you might be able to recommend me to be a governess or...perhaps help me secure passage to London."

"Would you be happy as a governess?" Harry asked in a skeptical voice. "You hated having a governess when you were young."

She gave a grim smile. "I fear I am out of options that would make me happy. That is no longer a factor in my decision. I am choosing which fate would make me the least miserable, and marrying Mr. Blyth is the worst fate of all."

Harry could hardly bear to hear her speak like that. Emotion swirled through his chest, concocting all sorts of ideas of how he might help her. Being a performer in London would be a life far different than the one she had always known. Her voice was truly special, but he hated the thought of her being treated as prima donnas were often treated and viewed by society. No one would ever know the truth about how pure and good her heart was. They would think she was a vain, attention-seeking wanton. Her mother was not such a woman, yet all the papers had written her as such a character. Emma's mother had abandoned that life for a reason.

"Do you dream of performing in London?" Harry asked in a quiet voice.

Emma was silent for a long moment. "No, I suppose not, but it is the best chance I have. I cannot go back to Tom and Arabella." She shook her head fast. "I will not."

"If not singing in London, then what do you dream of?" Harry leaned forward on his chair. The Emma he had always known was carefree and happy despite the misfortunes she had endured. Even the summer after she lost her mother, she was still full of joy and life, shining through her pain. Or perhaps it had been a facade.

Her blue eyes locked with his, a sadness hidden deep behind them. "It doesn't matter," she said in a hoarse voice. A weak smile pulled on the corners of her mouth, and it stabbed at his heart—the falseness of it.

He had always had grand dreams for his own life, including the future inheritance of the castle he now lived in. His uncle had never had an heir, so Harry had known for most of his life that he would one day inherit Garsley. Now that he was there, he had discovered a new dream—to transform the keep and gatehouse into a grand hotel overlooking the coast.

Such an ambition required money and a like mind.

He had gone to London for the last Season in the hopes of finding a woman with both of those things—a fortune that would help the dream come to fruition, as well as an ambition and excitement for contributing to the creation of the hotel. Miss Fitzroy had been the first lady to have both of those things, and so Harry had rather hastily solidified their union with an engagement pending her return from her trip to the Cotswolds. She would be coming to Garsley in approximately six weeks, and then they would be married. Love had not been involved in the decision. He had never been a romantic, yet since the engagement had become official, he was feeling the absence of love more keenly that he had expected. Shouldn't he miss her? Shouldn't he think of her often? In truth, throughout their entire courtship he had been more concerned with sending letters to Emma.

She was still watching him, that same sad, defeated look on her face. "Of course your dreams matter," Harry said, nearly standing to emphasize his words. "Whatever it is, tell me, and I shall do all I can to ensure it happens."

Emma shook her head. "That's impossible, Harry. You cannot give me my dream."

"Perhaps I can." He gave a cajoling smile, but her smile was gone, faded into lines of concern.

She took a deep breath. "You mentioned that I ought to bathe and change into something clean...?"

"Ah, yes." Harry cleared his throat, respecting her obvious desire for a change of subject. "I will send someone to search my mother's wardrobe and bring something clean for you to wear."

"Your mother is here?" Emma asked.

She had never met his mother. When Harry had spoken of his inheritance, he hadn't mentioned that his mother would be living with him. Emma must have assumed Mrs. Coleman would still be living with her eldest son, Harry's brother, Richard, in the manor he had inherited from his father.

"Yes," Harry said. "She prefers the grandeur of Garsley over the house I was raised in."

"I look forward to meeting her," Emma said, though her voice was nervous.

"I'll draw a bath, sir," Isabel said from the corner of the room. She curtsied and took her leave.

Emma twisted her fingers together. "Thank you, Harry. Thank you for everything. I'm sorry about how I—er—"

"Broke in to my castle? It used to be quite a stronghold. I suppose I will have to strengthen my defenses."

She laughed, a light trill that was as lovely and musical as her voice. The sound brought an instant smile to his face.

"One's defenses can never be too strong." She looked down at her hands, and the humor in her expression faded yet again.

Despite Emma's resistance, he was determined to find out what her dream was and how he might help her obtain it. If it wasn't to sing in London, then he would find something else that could make her happy. He wouldn't send her away from Garsley until he was content with her safety and well-being. He would have allowed her to stay forever living in one of the other towers, but he feared that the propriety of the situation would be questionable. And why should she spend her life locked away in a castle tower? She should be making a grand debut in London on the marriage mart, stealing the hearts of all the wealthy gentlemen in attendance. He knew she would. Perhaps when they had an opportunity to speak later, he would make that suggestion. Surely some of the funds allocated to the hotel could be spent on her Season. She was a dear enough friend that he would gladly be her sponsor.

He glanced at her face again, a heavy sensation of dread coursing through him. He had forgotten how lovely she was. How she lightened any burden he felt without saying a word. Feelings he had desperately tried to bury clawed at the surface.

He stood abruptly. "When you are well-rested, ask Isabel to direct you to my study and I'll give you a tour of the castle and introduce you to my mother."

A nervous look crossed her face, but she nodded. "I would like that very much."

Harry's prolonged study of her in such a vulnerable, and likely embarrassing state, must have been what made her so uncomfortable. Most ladies likely didn't enjoy being seen with dirt smeared on their faces. She must have forgotten how he had seen her in such a state many times during those summers at Stansham. There was so much more he wished to speak with her about, but at the moment he needed to leave her in peace. It was difficult, but he managed to take his leave with nothing more than a departing smile.

He wasn't quite certain what Mother would think of their unexpected visitor, but he prayed she would be cordial.

CHAPTER FOUR

W as everything at Garsley perfection itself? Emma had never tasted better water, nor better bread and grapes, and the bath she had taken had been the most divine of all the baths she had taken in her entire life. She could blame her high opinion of those things on the fact that she was starving and dirty and cold before, but that still wouldn't explain how she felt toward the owner of the castle. She had known her feelings toward Harry were strong, but she had hoped that she had found at least a little success in crushing those emotions since receiving his last letter.

She had not. The lock she had placed on her heart was more rusty and broken than the one on the keep door.

Rather than dwelling on that, she decided to blame her feelings on the fact that the only other man she had been interacting with had been Mr. Blyth, who was cold, calculating, and unsettling, where Harry was the opposite. As mortifying as it had been to have him happen upon her in the

41

keep, he had instantly put her at ease. She didn't have to wonder if she was welcome at Garsley. She felt as if she had come home. It would take all of her effort, but she would have to train herself to not love him. She could be fond of him, think of him as a dear friend, and esteem him highly, but any attraction she had to him needed to be stamped out. Her dream could no longer be what it had always been—to marry him one day. The very idea brought a blush to her cheeks. That was the dream of a foolish young girl, and as she had told him, it was a dream he could never help her obtain. Not anymore, anyway. Even if he wasn't engaged, he had never seen her as anything but his amusing friend, Emma. She had never had a chance.

She banished her thoughts of Harry for long enough to admire the room around her. The guest bedchamber had many characteristics of a castle, with stone structure and arched doorways, but most of the cold floor was covered in a large rug, and the deep walnut wood furniture added warmth to the space. The canopied bed was covered in fine red fabric with floral pillows, and she could already envision the space during the winter, flooded with heat from the hearth in the corner.

Isabel, the maid who had been most graciously helping transform Emma from a ragged rat into a presentable young lady, stood behind her as she secured the buttons on the back of the pale blue gown she had borrowed from Harry's mother. What would his mother think when she realized a strange young lady had broken into the castle and was now wearing one of her gowns? The thought made heat rise to Emma's cheeks. The dress was slightly large around the bust and shoulders, but it would have to suffice. How much could

Emma ask of their family? She didn't have any money to purchase new gowns, and she couldn't ask Harry to buy new clothes for her. That would be too great a favor. Once her white dress was washed, she would simply have to wear it every day.

Her hair had been washed, wrapped in rags, and was now dry and arranged in a pretty coiffure. Her face was clean, and the dark circles under her eyes had faded after her lengthy nap. She didn't want to hide away in her room all day, especially not after Harry had promised her a tour. It was already mid afternoon, and though her legs were sore enough to make her hobble, she still wanted to see every part of that charming old castle.

Isabel showed her to the study as Harry had instructed. The corridors were dark and mysterious, lit by rows of candles on the walls. The floors had been covered in wood, and several more wooden details covered the ceiling. Tapestries and framed paintings hung on the walls, and she could scarcely take it all in while limping along behind Isabel and her quick steps.

"The study, miss," Isabel said with a nod toward a large wooden door with iron details. She curtsied and went on her way, disappearing around the corner.

Emma took a deep breath as she stared at the door. In the silence of the corridor, she debated returning to her room. How could she convince herself not to love Harry? How strong was her will? She *knew* he was marrying someone else, yet her heart had still skipped upon seeing him again. It was simply unacceptable and unfair of her heart to do such a thing. She needed to tie it up and keep it restrained. She needed it to be as impenetrable as Garsley once was—with stone walls and a moat on all sides. She kept that image in her mind as she knocked three times on the door.

Harry opened it, and the moment his eyes met hers, the walls began to crumble to the ground.

Blast it all.

"There you are," he said with a smile. His light brown hair had a slight wave to it—tamed from the tighter curls of his youth. His brows, lashes, and eyes were all dark, yet warm and inviting. His smile caused an indent in his left cheek, one that could only be seen faintly behind the short layer of stubble that covered it. His eyes traced over her face. "Are you feeling better?"

Emma nodded, looking straight ahead at his cravat. Perhaps the first step to banishing her feelings for him would be to stop admiring the details of his face. "I feel much better, thank you."

"I'm glad to hear it." He waved her forward. "Before we begin the tour, I want to show you something." He stepped back, leaving room for her to join him in the study.

She walked inside, her nose flooding with the scent of ink and parchment. Bookshelves lined the walls behind a large desk and chair. The desk was covered in what appeared to be architectural drawings and maps.

He cleared his throat before picking up a pair of spectacles from the desk and setting them on his nose.

Emma stifled a laugh, unable to help herself. She had nearly forgotten about his spectacles.

Harry sighed, but his lips were smiling. "You have never ceased to tease me about these, but you must know I find it very impertinent and condescending."

"I'm sorry," she said, covering her mouth.

He grinned. "I know I look like I have aged fifty years, but not everyone can be blessed with perfect vision as you have been."

Her mind swirled with memories of hours of reading in the library at Stansham with Harry. She had always thought he was a poor reader, always misreading words and apologizing. But then one summer he had finally confessed to his need for spectacles, and he hadn't been ashamed to wear them around her ever since. In truth, she found them quite adorable. She would never, ever tell him that though.

"You don't look like you have aged fifty years," she said. "Only forty."

"Thank you. That makes me feel much more attractive."

Emma laughed, but the sound was cut short when Harry took the spectacles off and skirted around the desk toward her.

"Shall we see how they look on you?" He raised his brows. "I should like to have the last laugh."

"No!" Emma ducked and hurried to the other side of the desk, grimacing at the soreness of her legs.

He caught up to her easily, and she had no power to fight back as he took hold of her arm and turned her toward him. She caught her breath. When he had held her wrist in the keep that morning, he had seemed entirely unaffected by it. Meanwhile, her heart had been racing, much like it was now. She feigned nonchalance as she looked up at him. He slipped the spectacles onto her face.

She blinked, her vision suddenly blurred and distorted. "How do I look?"

Harry took a step back and started laughing, even going so far as to double over.

"You are atrocious," she said with a gasp. "Do I truly look so hideous?"

His laughter subsided and he strode closer again, carefully taking the spectacles off her nose and looking into her unobscured eyes. His face came into view, his eyes wrinkled at the corners with a smile. "Quite the contrary. I think they suit you."

"Do not lie to me, Harry George Coleman."

His jaw dropped. "You did not just refer to me by such a name."

"I did, and you deserved it." Emma laughed and swatted at his arm before thinking better of it. This was the sort of behavior they had always employed around one another— the sort of behavior her friend Lydia had called 'shameless flirting.' Emma had always denied it, but now that she was here with him, alone in his study—and knowing that he was an engaged man—she was far more aware of how her actions might be interpreted. Falling into old habits would not be wise.

Harry backed away from her swatting hand with a laugh, and she backed away a step at the same time. Silence hung between them for a few seconds before he placed his spectacles back on his nose. He cleared his throat awkwardly. He glanced at her face once before looking down at the desk. "I did not invite you in here to be mocked, so if you are finished, I will show you my designs." He placed the spectacles back on his face with a grin, daring her to tease him again.

Emma couldn't stop her smile. "I'm finished for now."

He gestured her forward to look at the drawings that were splayed out on the table.

She walked toward the desk. "What are they?"

"These are the plans for the gatehouse and keep." He met her gaze with a smile, the excitement in his eyes magnified behind the spectacles. "We are transforming them into a grand hotel that overlooks the sea. I saw you looking at the view from the keep window this morning. It is quite spectacular, is it not?"

"It is." It made her truly happy to see Harry take such ownership over the castle. He was thriving in it. When they were children and he had told her that he would be inheriting a castle, she hadn't believed him at first. But it was clear to see that he was always meant to be in this position. He would take something old and worn and turn it into something profitable and beautiful. He saw potential in everything, and he seemed unable to allow something with potential to fail. Was he proud of Emma for not settling for a life with Mr. Blyth? Or did he think she was a fool like Arabella and Tom did?

He pointed at one particular drawing. "The most grand rooms of the hotel will be in the keep, two on each floor, and then the gatehouse will have several smaller rooms." He pointed at a structure just outside the gatehouse. "This will be converted to stables where the guests' horses will be kept."

Emma's eyes widened as Harry spread out even more drawings of the planned interiors of the rooms. The furniture was exquisite, and not a single detail from floor to ceiling had been left out. "It seems you have every detail planned."

He laughed under his breath. "It has been my sole focus for the last year."

Emma hesitated, a frown tugging on her features. "You never mentioned it in your letters."

"That's because I wasn't certain I'd be able to make it happen." He paused, his jaw tightening as he looked down at the desk. "Until I met Miss Fitzroy, my betrothed, this was all nothing but an impossible dream."

Emma froze, her heart pounding in her chest. Now she had a name. *Miss Fitzroy.* Why did he seem so reluctant to speak about her? He had been so candid in his letter about his plan to marry. Those written words had sliced through Emma like a knife, as swiftly and painfully as they had come. Why did he seem to struggle to expound upon the details of his engagement now?

If Emma wanted answers, she would have to ask. She willed her heart and spinning thoughts to slow down. "How does Miss Fitzroy contribute to your plans for the hotel?"

Harry's chest rose and fell with a deep breath as he gathered up the papers for no apparent reason. He seemed to be looking for a distraction, a way to keep busy so he wouldn't have to look at Emma. "She has a large inheritance. She is aware of how it will be put to use, and she was quite eager about the idea. It is an investment of sorts for her, and she will also be mistress of the castle as an added benefit." He flashed a quick smile before it disappeared again. "She likes the idea of famous lords and ladies coming to stay at our hotel, and she has many ideas for how to furnish and decorate it. I think we will make a very good...partnership."

Emma watched him carefully, a chain of emotion encircling her throat. He didn't seem to be in love with Miss

Fitzroy. That was cause for the slightest bit of relief. But *shouldn't* Harry marry for love? He had always been so ambitious and not very romantic, so she couldn't say she was surprised that he had chosen this path. If his dream was to have his hotel and Miss Fitzroy could help him accomplish that, then he might be very happy indeed. Emma could not judge him for it. Since she couldn't marry Harry herself, she had even given up on her own dream of marrying for love. If she had the opportunity to marry any kind, respectable man who did not smell of beeswax and mildew, she would. Of all the paths she could take, marriage would be the best option...if only she had the opportunity to meet eligible gentlemen.

"With Miss Fitzroy's funds," Harry continued, "as well as my plans to obtain more investments from some of my other acquaintances, the hotel could be just as grand as these drawings depict."

Emma didn't know how to respond. Her tongue was tied for a long moment. "That...that sounds like a very effective plan." She cleared her throat. "When is the wedding to take place?"

Harry seemed reluctant to answer yet again, and it was obvious how he disliked discussing the subject with her. "That is yet to be planned. From Miss Fitzroy's last letter, she hopes to be at Garsley to begin planning the wedding six weeks from now."

Surely Emma would be long gone by then. She didn't know where she would go, but she needed to ensure she was not there when his betrothed arrived. "I must offer my congratulations. I hope your hotel and your marriage are a great success." She gave as polite a smile as she could manage before interlocking her hands in front of her. "Are you going to show me the rest of the castle?"

Harry snapped out of his grim expression. "Of course."

He led the way out of the study and down the corridor. Emma followed beside him, overly aware of how close his hand swung beside her own. "Many of the portraits you see have been here for generations," he said. "We added ours at the end of the row." He stopped and gestured at the wall where a portrait of Harry hung beside an empty space. He didn't mention who the empty space was reserved for, but Emma could easily guess. It drove a pang of grief deeper into her chest. She scolded herself for being so envious and followed Harry through the corridors until they reached the kitchen, dining room, and then the great hall.

Emma gaped in awe at the checkered floors and carved wooden details on the walls. Velvet chairs lined the sides of the room, and an enormous hearth stood at the end. "We have used this space as a ballroom," Harry said as he rotated to face her, walking backwards. His voice echoed. "Any music performed in this room is made to sound even better than it would elsewhere. It is some sort of magic." He beamed with pride as he stopped walking. "You should sing."

Emma scoffed. "Right now?"

"Yes."

"No." She laughed, pausing when she realized he was serious.

"Surely you must sing often. I found you singing in the keep this morning."

She shook her head. "*That* was not meant to be heard. It

had been far too long since I had sung, so I took the opportunity."

"Why had it been far too long?"

"Why are you asking so many questions?" She raised an eyebrow, suddenly uncomfortable. How could she explain that Arabella had forbade her to sing in the house? Harry pitied her enough already.

His smile was infectious as he still waited patiently for a reply. A third voice echoed from behind her, saving her from answering his question.

"Harry. Do you care to introduce me to your guest?" The older female voice was edged with curiosity.

Emma whirled around. At the opposite end of the great hall, a woman strode confidently forward. Her dark hair was mixed with strands of gray, piled elegantly atop her head. Layers of green taffeta skirts hung around her, and the waistline of her dress was slightly lower, taking after the fashion of the previous generation. The bodice was edged with lace, the elbow-length sleeves the same. As the woman drew closer, her sharp eyes and rouged lips and cheeks came into clear view. Her eyes were much like Harry's but, perhaps...not quite as warm.

"Of course, Mother, forgive me. As soon as the tour was over, I planned to make introductions." He stepped forward. "I believe I have told you about my friend from my summers spent at Stansham, Miss Emma Eastwood?"

Mrs. Coleman's expression lightened as she returned her focus to Emma's face. "Indeed you have. I had hoped to one day make Miss Eastwood's acquaintance."

Emma gave a polite smile, but something about the woman's stare was unsettling. "It is a pleasure to meet you,

Mrs. Coleman. I must commend you for raising such an exemplary son. There are few his equal." Emma hoped her words would be interpreted as friendly, with no detectable edge of longing.

Mrs. Coleman's response was nothing but a tight smile. Her eyes slid up and down Emma's figure. "I see you have helped yourself to my wardrobe."

Emma's face flamed. "I—"

"I hoped you wouldn't mind if she borrowed a dress," Harry said in a quick voice.

Mrs. Coleman's tight smile remained. "Not at all." Her brow twinged with confusion. Emma wanted to sink into the floor.

"What has brought you to Garsley?" Mrs. Coleman asked. "Harry did not tell me you were coming."

Emma opened her mouth in the hopes that something reasonable would come out. "I—I thought I ought to come to visit once before Harry's wedding." That was not what she had meant to say at all. She couldn't have Mrs. Coleman thinking that she wouldn't be welcome after he was married —as if there were some sort of romantic history between them. Emma's cheeks warmed as she searched for an alternative explanation that didn't include her eighteen mile walk and hiding in the keep.

"I see." Mrs. Coleman blinked twice. "Harry. May I speak with you privately?" Her smile was plastered on her face as she pivoted to face her son.

Harry exchanged a glance with Emma before giving a slow nod. "Of course."

Without another word, Mrs. Coleman turned on her heel and started toward the exit. Harry cast Emma an apologetic look as he followed his mother out of sight, leaving Emma alone in the great hall.

Shame tingled on the tips of her ears. She couldn't blame his mother for being unsettled about her presence there. He was engaged to a woman who would be arriving within two months. There was no room for old friends of his, especially female ones, to be taking any of his time. What was Harry going to tell his mother? How would he explain? Emma bit her lip nervously. All she could do was wait.

CHAPTER FIVE

Mother didn't stop walking until she reached the study. Once Harry had followed inside, she closed the door behind them. The clock ticked on the wall, filling the silence until she finally spoke.

"Well?" Her thin, arched eyebrows lifted. "Are you going to explain why you didn't tell me Miss Eastwood was coming to visit? I thought we had completed our list for the house party. There are no other ladies coming. Miss Eastwood will be quite out of place among the gentlemen."

Harry rubbed one side of his face. He had nearly forgotten about the upcoming house party, if he could call it that. Since finishing the furnishings on many of their guest chambers, he and his mother had decided to host a number of Harry's acquaintances he had made during the last Season. As it turned out, owning a castle garnered a great deal of attention. All five of the men he had invited were wealthy gentlemen who had expressed interest in investing in his future hotel. By showing them Garsley and allowing them to stay for a time, he had hoped to secure their investments.

Emma's arrival that day had completely distracted him. There was only a week before all his guests would arrive, and they would be staying for an entire month.

"I didn't think of that," Harry said in a flat voice. "*You* will be here. She won't be the only lady."

Mother sighed. "She will be the only *young* lady. For whatever purpose she is here, Miss Eastwood must complete her visit and return home before our other guests arrive. I will not have any gossip starting about who Miss Eastwood is and why she is here when you are engaged to Miss Fitzroy."

"I cannot throw Emma out of the castle." Harry shook his head with finality. "She is welcome to stay as long as she wishes. The circumstances surrounding her arrival here are most dire. I ask for your compassion and kindness toward her. She has been dealt an unfair amount of misfortune."

Mother tipped her head to one side, planting a hand on her hip. The furrows in her brow deepened. "What are these dire circumstances?"

"Both her parents, as well as her stepfather, have died. She has been living with her stepbrother and his new wife, but she is no longer welcome."

"Why is she not welcome?" Mother asked in a suspicious voice.

"I cannot imagine why." Harry shook his head with frustration. "She is a sweet, well-mannered young lady. There has never been anyone so innocent and delightful as Emma."

Mother's eyes narrowed at the edges. Harry cleared his

throat. "My point is that I am certain her stepbrother and his wife are the only ones at fault. They gave her an ultimatum. They tried to force her into a marriage that was most disagreeable, so she planned to make her own way in London by auditioning to be a prima donna there."

Mother gasped. "A performer? Why would she ever choose that over marriage?"

"The man in question must have been vile, indeed. I think she made the right choice, but she was robbed of all her possessions on her way and could no longer afford passage to London. That's why she came here instead. She asked me to help her find a position as a governess or...help her secure passage to London." Harry groaned. "I do not like the idea."

"Nor do I." Mother's nose wrinkled. "Does she even sing well?"

Harry gave a half smile. "Her voice is the best I have ever heard. She would, without a doubt, be given a place on the stage, but that future doesn't seem to excite her. She is resigned to it."

Mother paced to the window, her shoulders tight. "That will not do. A pretty young lady such as her with no guardian to speak of will be eaten alive on the stages of London. And her beauty would be wasted as a governess." Mother paused, a hint of suspicion entering her voice again. "When you spoke of Miss Eastwood in the past, you never mentioned she was so talented and pretty."

Harry shifted uncomfortably. He had never liked to think of Emma as 'pretty.' Year after year upon visiting Stansham, he had admittedly noticed how she grew in beauty. At twelve years old when they had first met, she had been a small, scrappy thing with wild blonde hair and round cheeks. She had grown up, but the change was so gradual that he had hardly noticed her beauty until it was right in front of him.

He hadn't stopped noticing it since.

"It didn't seem the most important thing to tell you about her," Harry said with a shrug. There was so much more to Emma than her talent for singing and the physical beauty she had grown into. She was kind and witty and strong. What woman would walk eighteen miles through the woods on her own? He smiled in bewilderment.

"She is penniless, I imagine?" Mother asked.

Harry nodded. "It would seem that all she owned of value was stolen."

Mother *tsked*, shaking her head. "Poor girl. But I confess she is also a stupid girl. She should never have fled on her own. She should have married the man her stepbrother intended for her."

Harry's defenses rose. "It is unfair to call her that. You don't know the hardship she has endured, and you cannot begin to understand it."

Mother's eyes flashed dangerously. "Women do not have the freedom that you do. Marriage is the only way for a woman to maintain any respect in society, and Miss East-wood should have seen that."

"What am I to do?" He raked a hand over his hair. "Am I to sponsor her for a Season in London? If finding a husband is the best option for her, and her stepbrother will not give her the opportunity to meet any other eligible men, then I'm sure I could spare the funds."

"You most certainly cannot." Mother scoffed. "Every

spare penny you have is allocated to the hotel. To send Miss Eastwood to London with all the gowns and subscriptions and lodging expenses would be to sacrifice several of the furnishings."

Harry set his jaw, crossing his arms. "Emma's well-being is worth more than a few armchairs and rugs."

"She is not *yours* to provide for." Mother took a step toward him, eyes narrowed. "Do not be forming any ideas to the contrary."

"I don't know what you mean." Harry held her gaze, daring her to elaborate on her hidden meaning.

"You are engaged to Miss Fitzroy. Having a pretty, unattached lady in your care who is so dear to you is not going to bode well for your success."

Harry released the breath in his lungs as his heart gave a distinct thud. She *was* dear to him. She might have been *too* dear to him. He swallowed. "I am not going to betray Miss Fitzroy and the promise I have made to her, not under any circumstances. I have always done my best to behave honorably in any situation. That honor must extend to how I choose to help Emma out of her plight. She is my friend. She trusted me enough to come here when she had no where else to turn. I will not disappoint her."

Mother was silent for several seconds. "Did she know you were engaged before she came here?"

"What?" Harry scowled. "Yes, she did."

"Are you certain she hasn't come in the hopes of ensnaring you?"

"I'm certain." Harry's patience was wearing thin. If Mother had seen how Emma had mocked him for his spectacles or teased him relentlessly over the years, or how completely unromantic their relationship had always been, she would not be so skeptical. Harry was confident that Emma had never viewed him as anything but a friend, and she had not come with any of the sinister intentions Mother had mentioned.

"Very well." Mother adjusted the pendant at her neck absently, looking heavenward. "I will not assume the worst of her. But I still do not think she should be present when our guests arrive. You have one week to figure out what is to be done with her."

Harry's mind spun. One week was not nearly enough time. The London Season had just ended, and the next would not begin until the fall. If Emma was to make a respectable debut, she couldn't spend the months leading up to the Season living alone in London. She would need to be kept in his care until he could find her a respectable chaperone to accompany her at the start of the Season.

Mother turned toward the door, but Harry stopped her. "That is not your decision to make. This castle belongs to me and I may permit Miss Eastwood to stay for as long as she likes. If I am to send her to London for the next Season, she will need a safe place to live in the meantime."

To his surprise, Mother laughed, throwing her head back and placing a hand on her forehead. "Oh, Harry, your ambitions are often too much. Do you truly believe your new wife will be so accepting of your young female friend living within these walls? You will be long married by the time the Season begins."

He hated to admit when Mother was right. "Do you have an alternative solution then? One that doesn't include sending her out to the streets alone?"

Mother gave an impatient sigh, placing one hand on the door handle. "There is one idea, but I'm not entirely certain I like it."

"What is it?"

Mother cast her gaze upward in thought once again before her attention returned to Harry. "We may not be able to offer her a Season with dozens of eligible gentlemen, but we could offer her *five*. That is still much better than the one option she had before. She doesn't have money, but she has beauty and talent, both of which can go a long way in stealing a man's heart."

Mother's meaning slowly sank into Harry's chest. "The house party? The five gentlemen I've invited?"

"The potential investors." Mother's eyes gleamed. She wanted the hotel to be a success just as much as he and Miss Fitzroy did. "They are all rather young and unattached, are they not? And wealthy."

Harry frowned, thinking about the status of each man one by one. "Yes, I believe they are."

"Then we shall allow Miss Eastwood to stay for the house party on the condition that she make a genuine effort to ensnare one of them by the end of it. In all propriety, of course," she added. "Surely she will find one who is to her liking, and if she is as flawless as you seem to believe she is, then she should have no trouble making him fall in love with her."

Harry glowered at the desk as the idea raced through his mind. The five men he had invited were new acquaintances. He didn't yet know if he could vouch for their characters. What if none of them were worthy of her? Vexation rose in his chest, but he pushed it away. This was the best plan he or his mother had come up with. Emma would surely be the center of attention among five single men. Without any other women to compete for their attention, it wouldn't be difficult for Emma to catch their interest. But why did the idea make him so blasted uneasy? He pushed the sensation away from his stomach.

When he failed to reply, Mother threw her hands in the air. "Am I not a genius?"

"You are, Mother." He forced a smile to his face. "I will present the idea to Emma and hear what she says."

"There is one more condition I would like to add." Mother lifted her chin. "I should like her to sing in the great hall on the night of our guests' arrival. If she is as talented as you say, then they will be quite impressed with our method of welcoming them to Garsley. It will help her catch their immediate attention as well. We will make it clear that she is not a hired performer, but a friend."

"If Emma accepts, then yes."

"And we are still planning to keep your engagement a secret from the investors, yes?"

Harry nodded. He had decided it would be best to avoid questions about his upcoming marriage and Miss Fitzroy's dowry. If the investors liked the idea of the hotel, they might be prompted to stake more money knowing that the plans required it. The more grand it could be, the better their profits would be in the end. He would take every penny he could.

"Then you must inform Miss Eastwood of the secrecy of the matter before the men arrive," Mother added.

"I will." His chest felt empty as he imagined the coming weeks. How would it feel to see Emma interacting so closely with the five gentlemen? It left a bitter taste in his mouth. "May I ask to add a condition as well?" Harry asked, facing his mother with a serious expression.

She raised her brows expectantly.

"I would ask that you make your best effort to make Emma feel welcome here. She does not deserve to feel like a burden any longer."

Mother scoffed. "I hope you don't think so little of my manners. I will treat her as I would any other guest." She paused. "So long as she doesn't cause trouble."

"Good. I will hold you to it." He gave Mother a quick smile before opening the study door and ushering her out. He followed her into the corridor, suddenly nervous about the prospect of presenting the plan to Emma. Would it feel like the same ultimatum her stepbrother and his wife had given her? In essence, she had no choice but to marry one of those five gentlemen before her time ran out at Garsley. She could always still go perform in London, but this was an opportunity to escape an uncertain fate. He hoped she would see the opportunity in it and not be frightened by the prospect. Perhaps she would feel a little of both.

"Where are you going?" Harry asked as he caught up to Mother's determined strides.

"To tell Miss Eastwood about her task."

"You may leave that conversation to me," Harry said in a quick voice.

Mother continued walking, shaking her head. "I think it would be better if she heard it from me."

Before Harry could stop her, she marched into the great hall.

CHAPTER SIX

At the sound of voices in the corridor, Emma quickly retracted her hand from the piece of armor she had been touching. It was attached to the wall just below a set of swords, the metal rusted and ancient. She interlocked her hands behind her back and stepped away from the wall just as Mrs. Coleman strode into the room. Harry followed closely behind her, a troubled look on his face.

Emma gave her warmest smile, but Mrs. Coleman's demeanor was serious. "Miss Eastwood, I'm afraid my initial greeting was not as welcoming as I would have liked it to be. Now that I know your purpose in being here, I must sympathize with you."

A wave of relief crashed over Emma's shoulders. At least Mrs. Coleman now knew why Emma was wearing her dress. "Thank you. I am very sorry for coming so unexpectedly."

Mrs. Coleman's lips curled into a pursed smile. There

was a smudge of rouge on her teeth. "It is no matter. The timing is actually fortuitous for your sake. Harry and I have been discussing what we might do with you."

"*Do* with me?" Emma squeezed her fingers anxiously.

Harry stepped forward. "We have an idea, that is all, that might secure your future well-being." The solemn look on his face was far from comforting.

"Yes, that is what I meant." Mrs. Coleman's features twisted in annoyance as she turned away from her son. "He has told me of your plan to travel to London to audition to be a performer. Is that correct?"

Emma gave a weak nod.

"Well, I am of the opinion that such a path is not suitable for a genteel young lady such as yourself. It has come to my attention that you have not had the opportunity to meet many eligible young gentlemen in your home town?"

"I have not. There is only one unmarried young man in the entire town, in fact."

"A tragedy for any young lady." Mrs. Coleman gave a dramatic sigh. "If I had been your guardian, I would have sent you to the marriage mart in London a long time ago. How old are you?"

"Three and twenty."

Mrs. Coleman's nose wrinkled. "Yes, that is far too old not to have had such an opportunity."

Tom had never been able to afford a Season for her, or at least that was what he had said. As soon as Arabella came into his life, expending such funds on Emma was even more out of the question. "My stepbrother could not afford it."

"Unfortunately neither can Harry," Mrs. Coleman

continued. "All the funds our family has and will procure in the near future have been allocated to the building of the hotel. Not to mention that the Season does not begin until the fall and Harry will be married before that. I hope you will understand that his wife would not like you to be living here during their time as a newly married couple."

Emma could sense Harry's frustration building. She looked down at the floor, suddenly unable to look at him. She could feel his gaze on her face. "Of course! That is completely understandable. I would never have asked for such an expense to be taken on my behalf." For Harry to fund her Season was preposterous. She never would have made an assumption like that.

Mrs. Coleman drew a step closer. "However, there is a way for you to meet five eligible bachelors without any such expense."

Emma's brows shot up. "How?"

"That is the good timing of your arrival. Harry has not mentioned it yet, but we had a house party planned for five wealthy, unattached acquaintances of his from London to join us at Garsley. They are interested in investing in the hotel, and the more investors we have, the more grand it can be." She gave a light laugh. "We wanted to offer you the opportunity to stay for the month of the house party on the condition that you are willing to sing for our guests upon their arrival."

"That condition was my mother's, not mine," Harry interjected. "The entire idea was, in fact, hers." He apologized with yet another glance in Emma's direction. "You don't have to sing if you don't wish to. And you are welcome to stay regardless of your efforts to secure a husband." He shot his mother a pointed look. Emma had never seen him so vexed. He hid it well, but it was clear that his mother had phrased the idea differently than he would have.

"I thank you for the opportunity." Emma's heart pounded. Singing for a few guests would be better than being sent out onto the streets. A month would give her plenty of time to plan what to do next. She could begin looking at the papers for any open governess position, and if she was lucky, one of the gentlemen might be a good match for her.

Mrs. Coleman carried on, ignoring Harry's interruption. "It is up to you, Miss Eastwood, if you will have the wisdom to take this opportunity to select a husband from among the party. After it is over, Harry will begin wedding preparations and it will not be prudent to have you here. He is too kind to say so, but I will not hide the truth from you." She smiled, though her words were heavy.

Emma took a deep breath. Mrs. Coleman was right. This was the best chance she was ever going to have. If she went to London to live alone and perform on stage, she would no longer be eligible to marry a respectable man, unless by some miracle she had the luck her mother had with Emma's father. Emma's reputation would be ruined and her morality would be openly called into question. If she could manage to find a man from among the party who was half as good as Harry, she would be pleased.

"That is a very generous offer, Mrs. Coleman. I-I will do my best to make a good impression on these gentlemen during their stay." Determination rose in her heart, but also nervousness. Five bachelors in one house? Being the only single young lady would be daunting, to be sure.

"You will have to present yourself well, of course," Mrs. Coleman continued. "I will ensure you are well prepared to behave with the manners that will be expected of you. You may have to employ a little flirting and romancing, but I think it should be no great task to ensnare one of them by the end of the month. Any of the five men could provide you with a very comfortable, safe life away from the critical eye of the London stages."

The pressure she would feel was worth enduring if she could have a chance to meet gentlemen besides Mr. Blyth. Anyone would seem wonderful in comparison, she was sure of it. Her gaze flitted to Harry, and her stomach sank.

If he was nearby, would anyone truly seem wonderful? She highly doubted it. "Thank you both very much for this opportunity. I will not waste it." Emma's mind spun. How could she ensure these men were impressed with her? Her singing on its own could not win her a husband. She would need to be charming in many other ways as well. She would need to flirt and encourage their affections. How on earth was she supposed to do that? Her friend Lydia had accused her of flirting with Harry, but his affections had never been encouraged by it. How could it work on one of these five strangers?

"I am glad you are willing to pursue the task," Mrs. Coleman said, clasping her hands together. "I suggest you begin preparing." She paused, her eyes sliding all the way down to Emma's toes. "I should like my dress back as soon as you are finished with it. And you will certainly need more dresses if you are to impress these gentlemen."

Emma's stomach twisted with panic. She couldn't ask Harry to provide her with new dresses. It was too much that she was already staying there for an entire month. "The dress I wore here is being washed. Perhaps with a variety of ribbons none of the men will notice?"

Mrs. Coleman stared at her with no small measure of dismay. "I will take you to the modiste tomorrow to be fitted for several new dresses. That is an expense that I'm afraid is necessary to take." She grimaced, and a pang of guilt dug into Emma's stomach.

"It is not a great expense," Harry said in a reassuring voice. "I am happy to provide you with new dresses." Each time he glanced at his mother, the vexation returned to his features. It was clear that he didn't approve of many of her choices of words.

"Yes, well, I think it will be a wonderful time." Mrs. Coleman gave a stiff smile. "Again, what a pleasure to meet you, Miss Eastwood. If you have any questions about formalities or flirtations or manners, please do not hesitate to come to me for assistance."

"Thank you," Emma said, though she was already certain she wouldn't be going to Mrs. Coleman for advice about manners. Emma didn't want to emulate her behavior if she was going to try to secure a husband. There was something in Mrs. Coleman's expressions and words that made her seem false. If Emma was to catch any man's attention, she would need to be genuine and personable. And, she couldn't forget *flirtatious*. Her stomach gave another nervous flop.

Mrs. Coleman left the great hall, leaving Emma alone

with Harry once again. She could scarcely grasp onto her thoughts for how quickly they were whirring through her head. "I will leave at once if I will be any sort of inconvenience," she blurted in the silence.

Harry shook his head, striding toward her. He looked far too handsome in his casual waistcoat and shirtsleeves. His cravat was loosened, his eyes flooded with kindness. "I own this castle. It is not my mother's," Harry said. "If I say you are welcome, then you are welcome. Do not pay any heed to her...implied ultimatums."

Emma wanted to believe him. Tom had said the same thing shortly after marrying Arabella. It hadn't taken long for Arabella to convince him that Emma was a pest who deserved to be cast out. Would Harry's resolve falter just as quickly? She looked into the warmth of his eyes, and her doubts settled. She had never known him to be fickle. Once his mind was made up, it was made for good. If he said she could stay, then she could stay. If he said he would marry Miss Fitzroy, then he would. If he said he would build that grand hotel, then it would be done. He was reliable in that way.

She loved it and hated it at the same time.

"It is true what she said," Emma said in a quick voice. "Once you are married I won't be able to stay here. I ought to take the opportunity to find a husband among your guests quite seriously."

Harry's throat bobbed with a visible swallow. "I agree. That would be the best thing for you to do."

Silence fell between them again, and she could hardly bear the awkwardness of it. "I only have one week to prepare." She paced toward the wall and back again, momentarily forgetting the soreness in her legs. "Will you help me? I don't have the slightest idea of how to...woo a gentleman."

Harry chuckled, watching her with crossed arms and a curious look. "I assure you, you have a better chance of wooing a gentleman if you do not *try* at all. Such obvious efforts are often more repelling than they are alluring."

"You see? These are the things I do not know. I need a pencil to write all of this down." She brushed a loose curl off her forehead with a sigh. "If I can't *learn* how to attract a gentleman, then what do you suggest I do?"

Harry shrugged. "Simply act like Emma Eastwood." A wry smile pulled on his mouth. "That is enough, I promise." She stopped pacing, a distinct flutter erupting through her chest. Harry's dark lashes shielded his eyes from view as he looked down at the floor. "Do not trouble yourself over your manners or behavior. I suspect all five men will be smitten from the moment they hear you singing. I will ensure they all know you are unattached and in search of a husband."

Emma wanted to feel grateful, but instead she felt hollow. She wasn't unattached, not really. "All I ask is that you do not tell them the more embarrassing things about me," she said, hoping to lighten the air between them.

Harry raised his eyebrows with a grin. "Such as...?"

She gave him a pointed look. "My snorting abilities."

A laugh burst out of him. "That was not on my mind until now, so I must thank you. I will be sure to add that to my list of recommendations when I speak about you to the gentlemen."

She glared at him. "I should not have reminded you."

"Hmm, I don't think you've done enough to remind me, actually. Will you please demonstrate?" He inched closer, that blasted dimple sinking deeper in his cheek.

Emma skirted away, shaking her head as her own laughter spilled out. "As you know, I only demonstrate the talent when I am in the company of swine."

"Perhaps you will soon realize that the gentlemen are swine. Will you demonstrate then?"

"I suppose if they prove themselves to be akin to pigs, then I shall have nothing to lose by displaying my snorting talent."

"You didn't hesitate to display your *talent* in front of me when we visited the farmers and their pigs at Stansham."

"I was not trying to catch *you* as my husband, so I had no hesitation."

Harry gave a half smile before looking down at the floor again. "That was certainly never my suspicion."

What did he mean by that? Her heart picked up speed. She had only been so carefree because she was comfortable with him—more so than she had ever been with anyone. She had never hinted at her feelings because she had been terrified of ruining the joy that it was to see him each summer. If he had known she liked him, she wouldn't have been carefree around him at all.

She halted her thoughts. It didn't matter. If she allowed herself to be distracted by her wayward feelings for Harry then she would never accomplish her objective. Her focus needed to be on the five gentlemen who would be arriving the next week. She needed to come to know each one. No one could be excluded. Once she had decided which of the five was the best match for her, she could expedite her efforts.

It was daunting, but not nearly as daunting as the reality that Harry would be there to observe the entire thing. Even at that very moment, awkwardness was suspended between them.

"Shall we finish your tour?" Harry asked finally.

Emma gave a grateful nod. "There is still so much to see."

He led her to the library next, which was almost as impressive as the great hall. The collection of books was sparse, but she was certain that Harry would fill the shelves by the end of his life. Next, they went past all the floors of bedchambers, the music room, and drawing room. After that, they walked to the courtyard and stables, each of the corner towers, and back to the keep and gatehouse. Harry explained a few of his ideas for the hotel, waving his hands excitedly as he gestured at each part of the keep. His eyes lit up as he spoke of his dream, and Emma found herself quite envious.

What would she give to have such a passion for anything besides him?

She would have to learn how. She would have to find something that excited her the way Harry's hotel excited him, or how singing on London's stages had excited Mama, or how fine fabrics and jewelry excited Arabella. Emma had been living her life the last several years only with anticipation of seeing Harry again, or of receiving another of his letters. What else could she look forward to now that everything would change?

She needed to fall in love with one of those five gentlemen. If she set her mind to it, surely her heart could change. She might find something new to dream about after all. She would have to become a little more like Harry if she hoped to secure one of those men.

She would have to become frightfully ambitious.

CHAPTER SEVEN

"I've ne'er seen a modiste work so quickly," Isabel said as she finished fastening the back of Emma's new gown. The budget Harry had given her had been far too generous. Emma had ordered several new dresses, and two were already finished.

Over the last week, Mrs. Coleman oversaw all the details of Emma's day like a hawk, watching her every move. If Emma went for a walk on the grounds, or took a book from the library to read, Mrs. Coleman was eerily aware of it. It was almost as if Mrs. Coleman had instructed servants to spy on her. The thought sent a shiver over her shoulders. Emma had spent as much time with Harry as she could, no matter how painful it was. They had started reading a book together. She had bested him in chess three times, and piquet twice. She hadn't counted the times he beat her; she chose to focus on the fact that she won more often than she lost. Mrs. Coleman didn't seem to like Emma's interactions with Harry, and she put an end to them as often as she could, inviting Emma to join her for tea and embroidery instead.

Mrs. Coleman was right to keep Emma away from Harry. Emma apparently lacked the strength to do it herself. She had told herself she would keep her distance, but she had found it impossible. Perhaps it would be easier once the bachelors arrived...

...that evening.

All day, Emma had been in her room for hours, singing and rehearsing the song she planned to perform for the guests that evening. It was her favorite piece her mother had sung for her each time she requested it, and though she had been practicing it all her life, she was still nervous for her performance. From her room, she had heard the men arriving one by one. Their voices had been muffled, but she suspected that everyone had found their way to their rooms on the floor above her by now. Emma's hair was still yet to be arranged, but at least she was dressed.

She admired the pink satin of her gown and the white gloves that extended up above her elbows. Isabel had applied a thin layer of rouge to her lips and pinched her cheeks rather excessively to give them a little ruddiness.

By the time her hair was arranged and the necklace Mrs. Coleman had lent her was draped around her collarbone, Emma hardly recognized herself. She hadn't had a reason to be so elegant in a very long time, if ever. The curls hanging at her temples were perfectly shaped, a look she had never achieved with the help of any other lady's maid. She took a deep breath as she finished taking in her reflection. Could she really do this? Could she impress them? Her hands shook as she adjusted her gloves.

"Ye look radiant, miss." Isabel's eyes gleamed with pride at her work as she made one more circle around Emma. Isabel's dark, straight hair stuck out the front of her cap on both sides, but she tucked the strands away from her eyes to see more clearly. "I'm 'fraid you might start a war 'mong these gen'lemen."

Emma laughed, but stopped herself. "How do you know about—" she paused. "Did Mrs. Coleman tell you?"

Isabel gave a shy nod. "I know everythin,' miss."

Emma would have to take care with what details she told Isabel. Anything she said would likely go straight to Mrs. Coleman's ears. "I think you did fine work. I hardly recognize myself." Emma took another shaky breath. "Thank you."

Isabel curtsied and took her leave of the room. Emma was expected in the great hall in less than five minutes. Her heart raced, but she squared her shoulders and held her chin high. She needed to appear confident and desirable. She couldn't afford to be timid or forgettable.

Before she could lose her nerve, she strode out into the corridor.

Harry tapped his foot nervously on the checkered floor. His guests had all arrived and were sitting on the velvet chairs in front of the fireplace where Emma would stand to sing. The five gentlemen had arrived on time and had been shown to their rooms prior to dressing for dinner. Emma was not the only one who needed to impress these men, although, she would be impressing them in a much different way. Harry had to impress them with his castle—with the potential that it held. The tour of the keep and gatehouse were scheduled for the next day, but until then, he still needed to be an excellent host.

Mother was already seated as well. Emma was the only one missing. After a long day of travel, the gentlemen were hungry and eager to begin the meal.

Perhaps he should have planned Emma's performance for *after* dinner.

Fortunately she didn't keep them waiting for long. His ears caught the sound of quiet footfalls from behind them. He turned around in his chair, and his breath hitched temporarily in his chest. Emma stood at the back of the great hall, gloved fingers fidgeting at her pink satin skirts. The moment her eyes met his, an unfamiliar flutter swooped through his stomach. Her hair, skin, and satin dress shone in the candlelight, and the bashful smile on her lips added to her charm. She lifted her chin and released the sides of her skirts as she walked forward. She looked beautiful and regal, and it took him a moment to realize he should be standing.

He hurried to his feet and turned to address the other guests, who were following suit. "Gentlemen, allow me to present Miss Emma Eastwood, a dear friend. Miss Eastwood will be favoring us this evening with a musical performance before we make our way to the dining room."

The five gentlemen watched Emma as she gave a polite curtsy and then made her way to the front of the room. He would save their introductions to Emma until after her performance. Of the five of them, Harry had already ruled out at least two as candidates for Emma's husband. By his own opinion, anyway.

He had known all of them briefly in London, but now that he was viewing them as potential husbands for Emma, his vantage point was much different. One of the men, Mr. Dudley, had spent at least ten minutes discussing his newest telescope and each of the different constellations he had mapped out in his spare time. There was certainly nothing wrong with having a passion for astronomy, but Harry already knew that Emma would quickly grow bored with such conversation. Another man, Lord Watlington, was more advanced in years, though not entirely out of the question if Emma liked older gentlemen. Harry scowled. He didn't have the slightest idea of what preferences Emma had when it came to men.

He shunned his thoughts. It was a *good* thing that he didn't know. He shouldn't have been curious about it at all.

He focused on Emma as she took her place at the front of the hall. Mother followed her and sat at the pianoforte. She had been practicing the accompaniment all week.

The guests fell silent, obviously already taken with Emma's beauty. Harry couldn't blame them. His throat was dry as he watched the signs of nervousness in her expression and posture. They were so subtle, and he was the only one in the room who knew her well enough to recognize them. To any eye less trained, she would appear perfectly composed. He was practically beaming with pride, hoping she would notice his encouraging smile, but then he remembered Mother's words. *She is not yours to provide for.* He looked around the room. Which one of the gentlemen there would be the one to do so? A sinking sensation started inside him, and it didn't stop as the music began.

Mother played the first notes on the pianoforte, and after two measures, Emma's voice joined the melody. She sang in Italian, and though he could only understand a few of the words, the emotion in the song cut straight to his bones. The tune was haunting and slow, but Emma's voice was clear and soft, every trill and note perfectly placed against the melody. She looked and sounded angelic as she delivered the message of the song as if she had been born to do so. Perhaps she had been. What if he and his mother had made a mistake encouraging her not to audition in London? They were depriving so many people of the privilege of hearing her voice. But if it wasn't Emma's dream, then it didn't matter. There had been a determination in her gaze when she had accepted the opportunity to find a husband from among the party of guests. Perhaps she belonged in one of their grand houses, singing only for their guests and her own children as her mother had sang to her.

Harry's heart ached, yet he didn't dare examine the reason, as the last notes of her song rang through the air. The guests erupted in applause.

Emma gave a broad smile, offering a bow as she accepted the praise. Harry wanted to rush forward to tell her how wonderful her performance had been, but he would have to wait for his turn. The five other gentlemen were already walking out of their rows to speak to her.

Harry hurried around them in order to be present to make their introductions. Emma had made the impression she hoped for, that much was certain. She could not have possibly made a better one. He managed to make his way to her side before the first of the bachelors could.

He leaned toward her with a smile. "That was beautiful, Emma, truly."

"Was it?" she asked in a timid voice. Her blue eyes landed on his.

"Yes." Harry straightened his posture as Mr. Dudley inched his way closer. Perhaps there would be time for conversation later, but at the moment, there were many introductions to be made.

As Emma met each of the men, she was polite and gracious, offering kind smiles that were sure to melt each of their hearts. Besides Mr. Dudley and Lord Watlington, the two men that Harry had already ruled out, there was Mr. Seaton, Sir Francis, and Mr. Hale. Fortunately all three men seemed to have something to offer besides their wealth. All three of them were younger, in their twenties or thirties.

Mr. Seaton was the loudest of the three, but had been polite during their various conversations in London and upon his arrival at the castle.

Sir Francis worried Harry simply because of his reputation when it came to women. He was a notorious flirt, but it was rumored that he was finally ready to settle down and marry.

Mr. Hale was friendly and amiable as far as Harry could tell.

Without knowing what Emma found attractive in a man, Harry couldn't say for himself which one she might have a liking for. He wasn't certain he *wanted* to know. There was a nagging pang in his chest that had refused to go away ever since Emma had entered the great hall and captured so much attention from the bachelors.

It was a feeling better left unexamined. Harry had never thought about how he might feel if Emma were to marry, but he hadn't expected to feel so...

He stopped himself, shoving the emotion away before he could give it a name.

After all the introductions had been made, he led the group to the dining room. His mother had worked with the housekeeper to plan an elaborate menu to give his guests a proper welcome. Their first impression of the castle and those in Harry's employ was essential to his success in convincing them to invest in his plan. Without any investments, the hotel could still be built so long as Harry had Miss Fitzroy's contribution, but with more investors, it could be even more grand than he had ever dreamed. It wasn't too much to dream that his guests could even include royalty.

Emma was seated between Mr. Dudley and Lord Watlington during dinner, which was the last thing Harry would have chosen for her. It was only the first dinner of many, but he could see how nervous Emma was as she listened to whatever extensive knowledge about astronomy Mr. Dudley was spouting close to her ear between bites of roasted duck.

Harry tried to keep an eye on Emma and the conversation but he also needed to converse with his own dinner partners. Mr. Hale sat beside Harry, and he had already offered several compliments about the meal. His dark auburn hair was arranged neatly, and his green eyes were inquisitive as he regarded Harry seriously. "I am already thoroughly impressed with Garsley. Were the furnishings already updated when you moved here, or is most of that work of your own?"

"Thank you. A great deal of it was already here, but I have added a few things." Harry sat up straighter. "I have saved many of the expenses so that I may apply them toward the future hotel."

"That is wise. The castle holds a natural charm that cannot be bought. I think you have done well with the simplicity of this area of the house. Guests staying in an ancient seaside hotel will expect more...grandeur."

"To be sure," Harry said with a chuckle. "I look forward to showing you my plans and giving you a tour of the keep and gatehouse."

"I very much anticipate it." Mr. Hale lifted his glass with a friendly smile, taking a sip.

Harry studied the man's profile for a long moment before stopping himself in the hopes of not appearing strange. Was Mr. Hale a good candidate for Emma? He was the most pleasant to converse with. He didn't have any obvious flaws.

When the meal ended and the ladies, what few of them there were, withdrew to the drawing room, Harry had glasses of port poured for all of the men. Six men, including Harry, in one dining room drinking port together wasn't something Harry had ever experienced in his own home before. He had a responsibility to impress each of them with his business intellect and character. It was a great deal of pressure.

"I hope you are enjoying your time at Garsley thus far."

Harry drank a sip from his glass, regarding each of the men with a quick glance.

A rumble of assent passed across the table. That was a good sign.

"I've never stayed at a castle before," Mr. Dudley said, withdrawing a case of snuff and taking a pinch. He inhaled deeply before continuing in a nasally voice, "I should like to bring my telescope to one of the towers to look at the stars."

"You are most welcome to do so," Harry said. "I hope each of you will feel the hospitable efforts that have been made during your stay here."

Sir Francis gave a deep chuckle, bringing one hand to his chest. "I began to feel it from the moment Miss Eastwood took the stage to perform for us." His sultry smile was off-putting. Harry would have to warn Emma about him and his reputation. Harry was making so many notes in his mind, he could hardly keep track of them.

The other men smiled, nodding their agreement.

"You must tell us more about Miss Eastwood," Sir Francis continued, leaning his elbow on the table as he took a large swig from his glass. His golden blond hair fell over his brow. "Where did she come from and how did she procure such a voice? Is she a performer in London?" His bright blue eyes were already reflecting the signs of deep interest. It did not take a great deal to entice a flirt like Sir Francis, and Harry suddenly felt a surge of protectiveness. Did Emma know how to dissuade the advances of a man like Sir Francis? What if he tried to take advantage of her? He needed to know that she was a respectable young woman.

Harry met his gaze, willing his voice to be steady despite the unexpected anger bubbling up in his chest. It was confusing. Wasn't this the reaction they had hoped for? Emma had succeeded in impressing several of the men already, yet all Harry could feel was defensive and uneasy. He took a deep breath. "Emm—Miss Eastwood is the daughter of a gentleman and was raised nearby in West Sussex. She is unattached if that was a question on your mind."

Sir Francis chuckled again. "It was, indeed."

Harry watched as Mr. Seaton's shoulders bristled. Mr. Dudley began drinking his port much faster.

"I think I shall return to the drawing room," Mr. Dudley said, bustling out of his chair. His spectacles slipped down his nose but he pressed them up in one firm motion.

"As will I," Mr. Seaton said, setting down his empty glass and moving toward the door with long strides.

The other three men exchanged glances, but Sir Francis simply wore that same arrogant smile. He apparently didn't see Mr. Dudley or Mr. Seaton as any sort of competition for Emma's attention. The older Lord Watlington watched the race out the door with lifted brows, a disapproving gleam in his eye. "What might we expect in a house full of men with only one single young lady?" He scoffed. "She will not be left in peace."

Sir Francis chuckled under his breath, as if to agree with the statement.

And to take part in the execution of it.

Harry sat forward. "Miss Eastwood is under my protection here at the castle. If I hear of anything untoward happening, the man responsible will be sent away at once." He took a calm sip from his glass, expending all his energy not to cast a pointed glance at Sir Francis. His anxiety rose when Sir Francis's smile grew. He didn't seem deterred.

Why the devil had Harry thought this was a good idea?

Mr. Hale joined the conversation, his face set with determination. "I will do all I can to help. Miss Eastwood seems like a very amiable young woman and I am certain she deserves to have an enjoyable stay at Garsley without being pestered by the visiting gentlemen." He stood, and Harry was once again impressed with his character. Even so, the thought of Emma being just as impressed formed a deep pit in his stomach. What was wrong with him?

When the other men were finished with their port, Harry led the way to the drawing room, fighting the impulse to send Sir Francis flying out the main doors when they passed them. Harry's jaw was tight as he stepped into the drawing room. Emma sat on the sofa straight ahead, flanked by Mr. Dudley and Mr. Seaton. She had already spent the entire meal in Mr. Dudley's company, and he could tell by the stiffness of her smile that she was exhausted.

She held a book on her lap, and when Mr. Dudley attempted to turn the page for her, the book slipped out of her hands and landed on the floor in front of her. In perfect synchronization, Mr. Dudley and Emma hurriedly bent down to retrieve it.

Their heads collided.

CHAPTER EIGHT

Throbbing pain split through the side of Emma's head. Mr. Dudley let out a string of unexpected curses as he sat up on the sofa. It was surprising. She had thought his vocabulary only consisted of astronomical terms.

He held his palm against his forehead and the top of his head where his hair was receding, stamping his foot on the ground in front of him and squeezing his eyes shut as he endured the pain. His spectacles had fallen to the floor, but she didn't dare reach for them after what had happened when she reached for her book.

She pressed her own hand to her head, her cheeks heating with the horror of what had just happened. All the eyes in the room were fixed on her and Mr. Dudley. She could hardly feel the pain in her head with all the mortification that raged inside her.

"I am very sorry," she blurted to Mr. Dudley as he finally sat up straight again.

"You might have allowed *me* to retrieve your book, Miss Eastwood," he grumbled, touching his forehead gingerly. Oh, dear. His head came into view, and it was quite red.

"Forgive me." Emma grimaced as she saw Harry from the corner of her eye. When had he entered the room? Had he seen what had just happened? She wished the sofa would swallow her whole. These men were potential investors in his hotel—she couldn't be injuring them and giving them any negative association with the castle.

Her gaze rose to meet Harry's as he stopped in front of her. His eyes were flooded with concern in the candlelight. "Are you all right?" he asked.

Emma nodded, but the worry didn't leave his eyes. He looked entirely uncomfortable as he shifted toward Mr. Dudley.

"Please, do not make a spectacle of this, Mr. Coleman," Mr. Dudley said with a weak chuckle, waving his hand through the air. "Carry on with the party."

"Very well." Harry took an immediate step back, casting his gaze in Emma's direction again.

Blast it all, she was on the verge of tears. Had Harry noticed? A lump formed in her throat and she blinked fast. It had been a long evening. Between the nerves of her performance, the anxiety of making so much polite conversation, and striking Mr. Dudley with her own skull, her composure was close to spent. How on earth was she going to last all month? She had likely already ruined her image in the eyes of most of the gentlemen in the room by being so clumsy. It was only the first night, and she was already failing.

Harry seemed torn between acting indifferent and

kneeling in front of her to ensure she was truly all right. His brow contracted as he stared at her.

"I-I think I am going to retire for the evening," Emma muttered, blinking as fast as she could to keep the tears at bay.

She stood, her head throbbing as she gave a curtsy and fled the room.

Out in the corridor, the tears began to fall, but she wiped them away. Crying was not going to change her circumstances. She could try again the next day. It wasn't over, she was simply being dramatic. Even if Mr. Dudley was no longer interested in her, that didn't matter. She was not interested in him anyway.

Of all the men in attendance, he had been her least favorite.

She hadn't yet had the opportunity to become acquainted with any of the others, but she could only hope they would be able to make light of her head collision with Mr. Dudley by the next day and not hold it against her.

Of the other men in attendance, she had noticed that Mr. Hale had a deep, polite voice and striking green eyes. His dark auburn hair complimented his features well, and he was quite tall, which she liked. Sir Francis was also attractive, though he did seem a little too arrogant for her preference. She couldn't rule anyone out yet. Well, besides Mr. Dudley. Between his nasally voice, sparse tufts of hair, and condescending manner of speaking, she had already decided he was not a candidate, even before she had injured him.

She laughed through her tears. The strange reaction

soothed her wild emotions. She had almost made it to the top of the stairs when she heard a set of footfalls behind her.

"Emma."

It was Harry's voice.

She should have known he would follow her. She wiped away the last of the moisture on her cheeks, her heart thudding as she turned around. Would he notice that she had been crying? It was difficult to hide when her cheeks became splotched with red and her eyes became instantly puffy. But it was dark on the staircase. The only light was faint tendrils from the candles in the other rooms of the house.

Harry held onto the bannister at the base of the wide staircase, but then he let go and jogged up the stairs toward her. His dark brows drew together. Why did he have to look so handsome that evening? He made all the other bachelors look like a herd of cows in comparison. Some of them were handsome, but as far as she could tell, none of them had a heart like Harry's. None of them *were* Harry, so that detail alone meant they would never compare.

His green jacket looked more grey in the dim light, and Emma looked down at the lapels of it rather than meeting his eyes. "I'm sorry for retiring so early. I-I thought it would be best considering what I did to Mr. Dudley." Her gaze flickered up to his face. She didn't know what she had expected to find there, but the amused smile on his lips was reassuring. There was a gentleness to it that disarmed her.

"Does your head hurt?" he asked.

"Hardly to the extent that Mr. Dudley's does. My skull must be thicker."

Harry's eyes were soft, but his voice was brimming with laughter. "Or perhaps you tolerate pain better than he does."

Emma sniffed as she suppressed her smile, rubbing the tip of her nose.

"You really struck him solidly, didn't you?"

"I am perfectly capable of retrieving a book from the floor," Emma said in a defensive tone. "I didn't realize he would attempt the same thing." She winced at the recent memory. With Harry as witness, she would never be allowed to forget it.

"I think you were secretly trying to rid him of his spectacles." He leaned forward with a whisper. "I know you have never liked men in spectacles."

Emma groaned, but a smile split her face. Harry's talent for turning heavy things into light things had always been a comfort to her. It made any weight easier to bear, even immense embarrassment. "You are right. The moment he walked into Garsley wearing those horrendous things, I immediately ruled him out as a potential husband."

Harry laughed. "I suppose I never would have had a chance then."

She stared at his face, all humor and smiles, but it was the second time he had referred to his belief that she never would have considered him as a potential husband. Had she really been so skilled at hiding her feelings all those years? What might have happened if she hadn't been so secretive about them? Her mind spun with questions and regret, but she tucked it away. It was just a coincidence that Harry had brought that up again. Wasn't it?

"I'm only joking. I wasn't *actually* so superficial in my opinion of Mr. Dudley," she said. "I found him agreeable, though rather excessive with his conversation on certain subjects."

"Astronomy?" Harry asked with a raised brow.

"Yes." Emma smiled. "But I think now that I have nearly split his head open, I will consider myself disqualified from his romantic interest."

"That may be a good thing. He would never love you as much as he loves the stars in the heavens."

Emma looked down at the toes of her slippers sticking out from under her hem. "How should I ever expect to be loved more than the stars?"

"You should expect nothing less." Harry nudged her chin up with the knuckle of his forefinger until she met his gaze. Her lungs refused to function until he lowered his hand again. How could he touch her so casually and then carry on as if nothing had happened? Her entire world had tilted with that one touch, yet he was still standing firmly on the ground.

"Why did you follow me out here?" Emma asked in a quiet voice, suddenly shy. "You should return to your guests."

Harry seemed to remember that he had other guests, his expression faltering for a moment. "I wanted to see if you were well, and reassure you if you had any doubts about the events of this evening. You have charmed every single person in this castle. Do not doubt yourself."

Emma took a deep breath, wringing her fingers together. "But what if I don't continue to impress them?"

"You need to change your perspective," Harry said,

looking deeply into her eyes. "You should not be worrying about impressing them. Instead, ask yourself the question: 'how are *they* going to impress *me*?'"

Emma nodded, her hopes bolstered up by his words. It would be much less intimidating to view the situation as he had suggested. "It's so strange to think that my future husband might be sitting in that drawing room at this very moment." *Daunting* was more like it.

Harry's features settled into a serious expression, but he eventually gave a smile. "Yes. Very strange." He let out a short breath before retreating down one step, his brow furrowing. "I-I hope you rest well, Emma. If you need anything for your head, Isabel can tend to it."

"Thank you." She walked up two steps backward before turning away from him. She thought she felt his gaze on her back as she made her way up the staircase. It took all her effort not to turn around at the top to see if it was true, and she was proud of herself for refraining. There were five other men in that castle that required her undivided attention. Well, actually her attention *was* to be divided five ways.

There was not room for a sixth.

Spending time with Harry, having conversations with him was just so different than the attempts she had made to converse with the other men that evening. With Harry, it was like being inside the walls of that castle—secure and safe. With every breath she took within those walls, and in Harry's company, she could feel a deep sense of history.

History was meant for the past, and that was where she needed to keep Harry and her feelings for him. One of the other five men could be her future, and that was not to be taken lightly. The next day, she would try to remember what Harry had told her.

She would look closely at each gentleman and see who could manage to impress her most. If, by chance, any of them cared to try.

CHAPTER NINE

Emma tried to focus on the egg on her plate at breakfast the next morning, but she was more concerned with a different egg.

The one on Mr. Dudley's forehead.

The blue and violet hued lump protruded just above his eyebrow. The side of Emma's head was sore to the touch, but it hadn't bruised or become swollen as Mr. Dudley's forehead had. She could hardly look him in the eye as he joined the rest of the guests currently eating at the table in the breakfast room. It was difficult to avoid his gaze when he was sitting straight across from her. Lord Watlington was also sitting on the opposite side of the table, his attention completely stolen by the food on his plate as he ate hastily in silence, his grey-flecked side whiskers moving up and down.

Mrs. Coleman's dark curls shone in the morning light coming from the window behind her, and her sharp eyes kept flickering toward Mr. Dudley and back to Emma again. She chewed on a mouthful of berries, her thin brows arching with disdain.

Where was Harry? He hadn't come down for breakfast. She knew he had a meeting and tour planned with all of the gentlemen for later that morning, so perhaps he was preparing.

Sir Francis, Mr. Seaton, and Mr. Hale were still filling their plates at the sideboard. She sat up straighter as Mr. Hale walked away from them. Would he choose to sit by her? She looked up, meeting his green eyes as he examined the seating options at the table. How could she beckon him to one of the seats beside her? Was there something she was supposed to do with her eyes? Was she to flutter her lashes or give a coy smile? She spent too long thinking about what to do. He had already looked away from her and chosen the seat beside Mrs. Coleman instead. She felt the rejection like a dagger in her chest. Well, drat. She must not have made a good impression on him.

She rearranged her thoughts as Harry had instructed— had *he* made a good impression on her? She couldn't say. They had yet to even have a conversation.

Sir Francis and Mr. Seaton took the chairs on either side of Emma.

"Did you sleep well, Miss Eastwood?" Mr. Seaton's voice came quickly, as if he feared Sir Francis would be the one to ask her first.

She turned to face him, examining his features little more closely. Mr. Seaton was rather short, but with broad shoulders and arms. His dark, curly hair was endearing, along with the square shape of his jaw. His voice was a little loud, but that might have been because of the circumstances of having Sir Francis on her other side and his wanting to have the first word.

"Quite well, thank you. Did you enjoy your first night at Garsley?" She made her voice friendly, offering a gentle smile.

"Oh, yes," he said. "Your singing was my favorite part of the evening. I am confident in saying that I have never heard a voice so extraordinary."

"You are too kind, sir." Emma wished she could call a blush to her cheeks, but her skin remained cold.

"How can one woman be blessed with so many gifts?" That voice came from her other side, and she turned toward Sir Francis's wide, charming smile. His eyes were blue and framed in dark lashes, his sandstone hair intentionally mussed to match his loosened cravat. "To have such musical talent and beauty is a rare combination, indeed."

This time, Emma did blush. His eyes traced over her face with such intense focus that she could hardly concentrate on her own words. She had never encountered a gentleman who spoke so boldly. She heard a huffed breath of annoyance come from Mr. Seaton, and he began eating his breakfast at an alarming rate, eyes narrowed.

"Th-thank you," Emma stammered. She remembered to smile. What else could she say? Being complimented so openly was a new experience for her. Was she supposed to compliment him in return?

"Are you quite fond of music?" she asked instead.

"It is one of my favorite arts to consume," Sir Francis

said as he took a slow bite from his plate. "I wish I had a talent for it, but I'm afraid I am quite inept."

"Surely you have other talents." Emma gave an encouraging smile.

His smile grew into one that was a little too mischievous, and he leaned close enough that only Emma heard his response. "I do. I would be glad to show you a few of them if you are ever curious."

Based on his tone, she suspected there was some scandalous meaning behind his words. As any proper lady would, she pretended not to understand it. "You seem as if you might be skilled at fencing? That would be my first guess. Perhaps you will be able to prove me right at the tournament later this week." She picked up her glass as her face flamed, taking a large sip of water. Mrs. Coleman had written up a list of events to entertain the men while they were visiting the castle, and one of them included a fencing tournament in the great hall.

Sir Francis laughed under his breath, throwing her another flirtatious smile. "I will try not to disappoint you."

Her stomach turned with unease, but she looked up at his blue eyes again. Perhaps she was misjudging him. He might not have meant anything unscrupulous. He did seem to like her though, which filled her with equal parts terror and hope.

When everyone finished eating, the men dispersed, and Emma heard Lord Watlington mention the meeting with Harry and the tour of the keep and gatehouse. Soon, Emma was left alone with Mrs. Coleman.

Emma started to stand to leave, but Mrs. Coleman

stopped her. "Please, sit." She gave a slow smile, nodding toward the chair Emma had just abandoned.

Emma cast a pleading look at the door, but unfortunately it could not save her. She lowered back into her chair in silence.

Mrs. Coleman pushed her plate aside and waved a footman over to clear it. Then she interlocked her fingers on the table and leaned forward. The rouge on her cheeks sank into the wrinkles that were exaggerated by the harsh morning light. "I thought I should inquire privately about your thoughts on the gentlemen thus far. Has anyone in particular caught your interest?"

Emma had expected to be scolded for her mishap the night before with Mr. Dudley's forehead, so she was actually relieved by the question. "I think it is too early to say. All five of them seem agreeable, but I will have to spend a great deal of time deciphering each of their characters."

"Do not take too much time, Miss Eastwood." Mrs. Coleman's lips pursed. "Spreading your attention evenly between five men will be difficult. You must narrow down your selection as quickly as you are able."

Emma fidgeted with the fabric on her skirts under the table. "Well, I do think I would eliminate Mr. Dudley as a prospect."

"I would agree." Mrs. Coleman's face scrunched with a grimace. "I like your taste already."

Emma studied Mrs. Coleman's expression. At times, Emma felt that she was an ally, but there were other moments when she found her constant watchful eye intimidating and disconcerting. Why should Mrs. Coleman be anything but an ally in her quest for a husband? The sooner Emma found a man to marry, the sooner she would be gone. Mrs. Coleman had the same goal as Emma.

"I have planned a picnic for this afternoon," Mrs. Coleman said. "I would advise you to take that opportunity to...flirt a bit more. Whether you think a man is humorous or not, you must laugh at his attempts to amuse you. Maintain eye contact while conversing. I saw you look away from Sir Francis multiple times this morning. Be coy, but not bashful. A man does not desire a wife who will be inattentive and unresponsive to his attempts at wooing her."

Emma nodded slowly, struggling to take in all the hasty instruction. "I confess it is all rather overwhelming. Harry has made efforts to reassure me that I ought not to worry too greatly about impressing them."

Mrs. Coleman's smile twitched. "You are not to converse privately with Harry."

Emma frowned. "It wasn't—"

"You are *not* to be alone in Harry's company while you are staying at Garsley." Mrs. Coleman's voice had changed, hardening along with her gaze. "He is an engaged man and I will not stand for you *tempting* him in any way."

Heat climbed up Emma's neck and onto her cheeks. "Tempting?" She shook her head in confusion.

The smile was long gone from Mrs. Coleman's face, and her new expression was so intense that Emma wondered if it had ever been there at all. "If your design was to come here and seduce him out of his choice to marry Miss Fitzroy, it will not work. Harry has never wanted anything more than he wants his hotel. He could never want anything more than he wants that. Especially not you."

Emma scowled, her heart thudding at the harsh, accusatory tone of Mrs. Coleman's voice. "I assure you, I had no such purpose in coming here. I don't have any influence over Harry's choice to marry Miss Fitzroy. He is a man of his word, and he will marry her. He doesn't care for me as anything but a friend."

Mrs. Coleman leaned back in her chair, her features becoming eerily calm. "That is good. I expect those circumstances to remain the same."

Emma's throat was dry as she swallowed, nodding her agreement. "They will," she choked.

Mrs. Coleman seemed satisfied with that response, though her eyes still reflected a hint of suspicion. She was silent for a long moment as she studied Emma's face. Was she looking for a sign that she was lying? Emma could hardly remember a time she had felt more vulnerable. What if Mrs. Coleman could see Emma's emotions—what if she could see straight into her heart and soul and know that Emma was in love with Harry? That was a secret Mrs. Coleman could never discover. If Harry hadn't seen it yet after so many years, surely no one else could.

With a flick of her hand, Mrs. Coleman gestured toward the door. "You are excused."

Emma stood, eager to escape the room and the woman's shifting personality. By the time she reached the corridor, her legs were shaking beneath her. Why would Mrs. Coleman ever think that Emma was some sort of...seductress? Her heart hammered with a hint of anger. Was it because she had planned to be a prima donna in London? Had the mere idea of it given her this false reputation in Mrs. Coleman's eyes? Mama must have endured so much disdain in her profession. It was one Emma hoped to avoid if she could. She couldn't fail her opportunity. As much as she hated to admit it, she needed to follow Mrs. Coleman's advice that afternoon.

She needed to put her flirting skills to the test.

CHAPTER TEN

There were several things Harry would have preferred to be doing besides watching multiple men act like buffoons in their attempts to impress Emma.

The plan was working too well for his liking.

Harry had planned a tour of the grounds for his guests as well as a picnic that afternoon. After the meeting that morning, he was feeling confident about the potential investments from at least two of the men. Sir Francis was the most eager about taking part in the scheme, with Mr. Hale expressing a great deal of curiosity as well. The other three were skeptical about a few of the details, such as how they planned to advertise the opportunity to stay at the hotel and how the place would gain any good repute. Those were things Harry had yet to figure out, but he had to act confident that the seaside views would be reason enough to draw people in, and that word would eventually spread through the papers and word of mouth. For the first meeting though, he was happy with what had transpired.

His jovial mood had vanished quickly, however, as well as his fondness of Sir Francis and his eagerness to invest. At the moment, Emma was walking beside him, arm linked through his as the group made their way to the hill just beyond the castle. Two large picnic baskets had been placed there along with blankets for the guests to sit on.

Harry would have rather stayed inside. He blamed his sour mood on the heat of the day, but he knew the true origin was not as obvious. His vexation was springing up from somewhere deep inside him—recesses he hadn't ever dared explore. The truth of the matter was that he didn't like seeing Emma laughing and smiling with other men. That had always been his place. Each time he made her laugh, it felt like a gift—some sort of prize that he had won and would treasure. But there she was, laughing at every word Sir Francis said. Was it really so easy to make her laugh? Was Harry not unique at all?

His jaw tightened as he picked up his pace, trying to listen to the conversation she was having with Sir Francis. Didn't she recognize how arrogant he was? He was clearly a practiced flirt, but perhaps Emma liked that sort of behavior. She seemed to be demonstrating a great deal of it herself. She was constantly smiling, and her eyes were practically adhered to Sir Francis's face. Should Harry warn her about him? He hadn't liked the way Sir Francis had reacted when Harry threatened the group about his requirement for proper behavior toward Emma. Was he toying with her, or did he have genuine interest?

Harry's thoughts continued to spiral, his steps feeling

heavier as they made their way toward the hill. Mother had walked at the front of the group and was already at the top of the hill, waving down at them.

They passed a pond that was part of the property, and the nearby grass was soaked as they trudged through it. Harry's boots squelched with each step, and he watched with growing annoyance as Emma laughed with Sir Francis, lifting the hem of her pale blue skirts and prancing through the marsh with him. Walking just a few paces ahead of them, was Lord Watlington.

"Oh, my!" he exclaimed, stooping down to look at something on the ground. "Miss Eastwood, there is something you must see at once." He tore his hat from his head to have a closer look at the ground.

Emma stopped walking, moving away from Sir Francis's side momentarily. "What is it?" she asked.

Harry caught up to them, stopping at Emma's side before Sir Francis could return to it. She glanced up at Harry before returning her attention to Lord Watlington.

Lord Watlington stooped over and reached into the wet grass. When he stood again, a surprisingly large serpent was dangling from his hands, coiling it's grey body around his arm. "A grass snake!"

Sir Francis cursed and skirted away toward the hill, turning around only when he was several yards back. "Put that *deuced* thing down."

Harry knew Emma well enough to know that she wouldn't be frightened by the creature, though she *was* disgusted by them. Her eyes were wide with dismay as Lord Watlington nuzzled his face close to that of the serpent. It's forked tongue flicked out, narrowly missing his nose. "I have always had a love for reptiles. I have an entire room at my estate that has been converted into a terrarium for the creatures. I have collected a large variety of species for my own study and enjoyment, some of which are highly venomous." He gave a gleeful laugh. Prior to that moment, Harry had only heard Lord Watlington speak a few brief words, and never with so much enthusiasm.

Harry exchanged a glance with Emma. Her eyes were brimming with laughter, her lips twisting against a smile.

"Would you like to hold it?" Lord Watlington asked Emma, a hopeful gleam in his eye.

She took a step back, tripping over the back of her wet hem. Harry lunged forward to steady her, reaching her just in time to prevent her fall into the wet grass. He held fast to her upper arms, catching the soft scent of her rose perfume. How had he never noticed that before? Her blue eyes collided with his, a soft pink touching her cheeks.

Harry released his grip on her, and she steadied herself as she returned her attention to Lord Watlington. "Th-that is quite all right. I am not particularly fond of snakes."

Lord Watlington's face fell, his mouth flattening to a firm line. "I see."

Was a love for reptiles one of his requirements for a wife? It now made sense that he was more advanced in years and had never been married, even with his wealth and grand estate. Still holding the grass snake, he turned away from Emma and continued up the hill. Sir Francis took several steps to the side as Lord Watlington approached with the serpent, his lip curling with distaste.

Emma turned toward Harry, which gave him an instant wave of satisfaction. She had chosen to speak to him instead of Sir Francis. "What on earth does he plan to do with that snake?" she hissed in a whisper. "Why is he still carrying it?"

Harry laughed under his breath. "He wishes to bring it home to his terrarium, of course. Did you not hear what he just said?" he teased.

Emma's brows drew together before a laugh burst out of her. "Do you suppose that is really true? What will he do with it in the meantime?"

"I suspect he will name it and keep it in the dark corner of his bedchamber."

"What do you suppose he'll name it?"

"Emma, to be sure."

She scoffed. "It looks more like a Harry to me."

"On second thought, I think it looks like a Francis." Harry mumbled as Sir Francis hurried down the hill toward them.

Emma raised one curious eyebrow at Harry, her smile fading just as Sir Francis reached her side.

"I expect a profuse apology for your lack of gallantry in protecting me from that vile creature," she said to him with a laugh.

Sir Francis leaned closer to her. "Are you talking about the serpent or Lord Watlington?"

This time Emma's laugh was obviously forced. She shifted awkwardly. "I meant the serpent, of course. That is the only vile creature I have seen today."

Harry's opinion of Sir Francis was lowering more by the minute. Was insulting the other gentlemen his way of trying to put himself above them in her eyes? Surely she was wise enough to see through his arrogance.

Sir Francis chuckled, brushing a hand over his hair. He cleared his throat, his gaze shifting to Harry, who was still standing nearby. "Mr. Coleman, tell me more about how you became acquainted with Miss Eastwood."

It was a strange change of subject, and Harry had to collect his wits before answering. "We met as children. Our families had a mutual friend who invited us to visit his estate each summer."

"Was Miss Eastwood always so agreeable?" Sir Francis asked in an irksome voice.

"It is not in her nature to be anything less," Harry said. He scuffed his boot over the grass.

"I do not doubt it."

Why did the man's tone make Harry's skin crawl?

Ever since Emma had arrived, his mind had been playing tricks on him. *Tricks*, that was all they were. Not feelings. Not regrets. He looked at Emma again, her curious gaze fixed on him.

"Have you yet considered matrimony for yourself, Mr. Coleman?" Sir Francis asked as he swept his gaze over the structure of the castle behind them. "Garsley will be needing a mistress, will it not?"

Harry didn't want to lie directly about his plans to marry Miss Fitzroy, but he still didn't want the knowledge to become public. "I have considered it." Harry paused. "Have you considered your own?"

Sir Francis flashed a sideways smile, pausing for several seconds. "With the right woman, I would be very inclined to. I do not require a great deal in a wife besides a pretty face and good health. I have all the connections and wealth I could desire already."

Emma's eyes darted to Harry's. Was there hope in her gaze? Why was his stomach sinking at that response? He was going mad. That was all that could explain the discord between his logic and the sensations that had been occurring inside him all day.

He was behaving like a child. Sharing Emma's attention should not have been such a taxing ordeal. He shouldn't have been seeking any of it. His focus during that house party needed to be on his investors and the hotel and his upcoming marriage. He *wanted* Emma to find a husband from among his guests. If she didn't, she faced an uncertain future. He simply wished he could select the man himself. He would be content if she chose any of the men *besides* Sir Francis.

He simply didn't trust him.

That must have been the only reason he was feeling so upset.

Satisfied with that conclusion, he made his way up the hill ahead of them, no longer feeling the strength to observe any more of their flirtations. In fact, from that point onward, he would do all he could to avoid the entire ordeal. He could leave the matchmaking to his mother.

His mood continued to deteriorate as he listened to Emma's laugh. He scolded himself for being so vexed. He scowled at the ground. Emma was never his, and she never would be.

So why did it feel like he was being robbed?

CHAPTER ELEVEN

Though he had never been a strong candidate, Emma thought it was safe to eliminate Lord Watlington as a prospect for her husband. He could never love her as much as he loved his reptiles. At any rate, the thought of living out her days in an estate that she shared with several venomous snakes did not sound appealing in the slightest.

Mr. Dudley had already been eliminated in her mind as well, but that didn't change his attempts to spend time with her. Over the past several days, Mrs. Coleman had been trying to have at least two meals per day arranged with all the guests together, and there was usually one group activity each afternoon. They had played nine pins, archery, and blind man's bluff, which was her least favorite of the activities considering all the blindfolded men trying to locate her with their outstretched hands. Mr. Seaton had grasped her perfectly by the waist at one point, and she had caught him secretly peeking out the bottom of the blindfold to do so. She still shuddered at the thought.

As the days went on, Emma watched Mr. Dudley's bruise change from purple to green to yellow, and Harry's mood change from cheerful to quiet...to utterly waspish. He didn't join them for most of the activities, claiming that he had 'business' to attend to or architectural plans to arrange or furniture to order. If he did join them, he was usually in a sour mood, and there was always some excuse he made to leave prematurely. Emma wondered if Mrs. Coleman had spoken to him as well about keeping away from Emma. It hadn't been difficult for Emma to keep Mrs. Coleman's request of not conversing privately with him. Harry had not made it possible.

She missed Harry and his reassuring words. Her anxiety grew with each passing day. Sir Francis and Mr. Seaton were in constant competition for her arm each time the group ventured outside. In truth, she found both of them quite annoying, but she hadn't found an obvious reason to eliminate either of them yet. Sir Francis was overly flirtatious, which made her a little uneasy, and Mr. Seaton was rather serious and intense when he finally managed to steal her from Sir Francis's side. Mr. Hale would hardly speak to her, and his piercing green eyes watched her as if she were a reptile herself and she might bite him at any moment. He intrigued her, but perhaps it was only because he was the only gentleman not paying her any attention.

Well, besides Harry.

It was a good thing, she told herself, that he was keeping his distance. It helped her concentrate on the fact that he was not a candidate for her husband. But at the same time, it hurt, because she still wanted him to be her *friend*. Did he not care who she chose? Did he not have an opinion? He was being far too silent on the subject. Each time she had such thoughts, she shunned them. It wasn't his ordeal to fret over. It was hers. He was focused on obtaining investments from the men, not marriage proposals. She should have been more grateful that she was given this opportunity at all. Harry could have sent her out to the streets, but he had allowed her to completely interrupt the house party. Perhaps he was regretting that decision and he resented her for taking so much attention away from the hotel plans. Her heart ached at the thought that she might have become a burden even to Harry.

One morning, Emma arose early, her mind weighing too heavily to sleep. She wrapped up her braid in a spiral and secured it to her head with two pins before wrapping herself in her cloak. She ventured outside for a short walk around the grounds. The sun had just begun to rise, and the early morning air was more chilly than usual. A sea breeze rustled at her hair as she made her way across the grass and under the arch of the gatehouse. Light rain trickled from the sky, landing on her cheeks like mist.

As she passed the door of the keep, a creaking sound made her heart leap with surprise. The door opened. She jumped back just as Harry came into view.

He looked just as surprised as she felt, his dark brows lifting. He wore a waistcoat over his shirtsleeves, but his cravat was untied. His eyes were slightly puffy as if he had just been sleeping. "Have you come to break into the keep again?" Half his mouth rose in a smile.

"You've caught me." Warmth spread through her chest.

It had been far too many days since she had seen him smile. They hadn't had a private conversation since the men had first arrived.

She was suddenly self-conscious of her choice of attire. She hadn't expected to see anyone this early, but she should have known better after her first encounter with Harry upon her arrival at Garsley. Wrapping her arms around herself, she shifted on her feet and looked at the ground. How convenient it would have been if she could read his mind. He must have been avoiding her for a reason over the last several days.

"What has urged you to break in this time?" Harry asked in a teasing voice.

"I much preferred the hard stone floor to my warm, comfortable bedchamber. I came to see if I might sleep what remains of the morning there."

Harry laughed. "The view must be as beautiful as I'd hoped."

"It will make a grand hotel, to be sure." Emma secretly hated that hotel. He might not have become engaged to Miss Fitzroy if he hadn't come up with the idea. Even so, she still admired him for having such grand dreams. Her only dream at the moment was to somehow secure a future for herself that did not include ridicule and so much uncertainty. She didn't have room to dream of anything else.

Harry closed the keep door and walked toward her, folding a bundle of papers and tucking them in his waist-coat. "Are you going to reveal why you were actually wandering around out here at dawn?" He raised one eyebrow with grin. "Or is it a secret?"

"What is a castle without secrets?" Emma pinched her lips together, giving him a mysterious look.

His reaction wasn't as she had hoped. His brows drew together, his eyes hesitant. He was silent for a long moment. "I hope you will be cautious with your...interactions with the gentlemen here."

Emma frowned, watching the signs of discomfort in his features. "What do you mean?"

He finally met her gaze, his expression serious. "Are you keeping a chaperone with you during every interaction? I think it is still very important that you take every precaution to preserve your reputation."

A surge of anger rose in her chest, but it was mingled with amusement. Did he think he could ignore her for days and then give her a lecture about her reputation? It was ridiculous. Did he think she had turned into some sort of wanton only because she was staying at a castle with five gentlemen? Her skin flamed. "I was *not* on my way to visit any of your guests' chambers if that is what you are concerned about." She crossed her arms, hardly able to look at his face.

"That's not what I meant," Harry said with a sigh.

"Then what *did* you mean?" She lifted her chin, daring him to explain.

He took a deep breath, the furrow in his brow deepening. "I don't know."

"Yes, you do." Emma took a step closer to him, unwilling to let him escape. He had been avoiding her for days. It wasn't fair that he could get away with no explanation now.

His gaze snapped to hers. "I just—" he exhaled sharply.

"I just have never seen you behave the way you have been of late."

She gave him a confused look. "In what way?"

He rubbed the back of his neck, shaking his head. "Please forget I mentioned it. There is no need to dwell on the subject." He tried to step away, but Emma blocked him.

"Harry, tell me. Now." She gave an exasperated sigh.

His eyes settled on hers, and her stomach flipped. She had stepped quite close to him.

"I have never seen you act so...flirtatious." He finally spit out the word as if it were laced with poison. "It's alarming, that's all."

It took a moment for his words to sink in, but then a laugh burst out of her throat. "Alarming?"

"Yes." Harry looked up at the sky rather than at her face. A hint of color had touched his cheeks, and she found herself staring at it.

"What is *alarming* about my flirtations?" she asked.

"I already told you. It's because I've never seen it from you before," he grumbled.

She was quite enjoying the unrest in his expression. The fact that her flirting with the other gentleman bothered him was peculiar but fascinating at the same time. "That is because I've never been given one month, five men, and the task of persuading one of them to marry me. How else am I going to catch a husband if I don't try to encourage a man's affection? I don't understand why it vexes you so much. You have hardly been around to witness it."

He tipped his head closer to hers, crossing his arms. "I didn't say it vexed me."

"But you did say it *alarms* you." She gave a hard laugh.

"Your mother is the one who told me to flirt more."

Harry frowned. "You should not listen to anything my mother says."

"I don't always. She also told me that I was forbidden to speak with you privately, yet here I am." Emma regretted the words as soon as they escaped her mouth. She looked down at his cravat, just beneath his chin—she was suddenly afraid to see his face.

Silence fell between them for several seconds, the air tight with awkwardness. "Why would my mother forbid you to speak with me?"

Emma dared a look at his eyes. They were dark brown in the dim light, burning with curiosity and...something else. She didn't recognize the expression, but it sent a wave of butterflies through her stomach. "Did she not have the same conversation with you? I thought that might have been why you have been so...distant the past several days."

"I've been busy," Harry said in a voice that was a little too defensive.

"I understand." Emma pressed her lips together.

"But what did my mother say to you?" Harry dipped his head down, drawing her gaze back to his face. Emma took a small step back. She wouldn't be able to concentrate if he was standing so close.

"It doesn't matter. Please forget I mentioned it," she said, repeating his words from earlier when she had pushed him to explain himself. She tried to keep walking past the keep, but he stopped her, grabbing her forearm and skirting around her.

"No, no, you cannot escape so easily. What did she say?"

Blast it all. She was trapped. "It was entirely unfounded,"

Emma protested. "But she seems to think I pose some sort of...threat to the success of the hotel." She swallowed, her gaze darting away from his. Would he make her explain further? She desperately hoped not. She could already feel the heat creeping up her neck and cheeks. There was no way she would repeat the part about being a temptress. Harry was obviously not *tempted* by her at all. He was vexed by everything she did, it seemed, including her methods of trying to catch a husband from the party as they had planned. If he had some other method, she would gladly listen, but he was not suggesting any alternatives to flirting.

"You? A threat?" Harry's voice carried an edge of amusement. "Does she think you are here on some nefarious errand to burn my hotel plans and dissuade my investors? She always assumes the worst of people. I will have to speak with her."

"No." Emma groaned. "Don't speak with her. That is not what she meant." She took a deep breath. "It is something even more ridiculous than that."

He scowled. "What is it then?"

Was he truly so daft? Emma was growing more uncomfortable by the second. She wrung her fingers together, looking at anything but his confused expression. She didn't want to see what his face looked like once he understood. "She has the idea in her head that I might...that I might be a reason for you not to marry Miss Fitzroy." Emma's words spilled out faster, leaving no pause. "As I said, it is ridiculous, but that is what she believes. As it is, I don't think there is any harm in you and I speaking privately since we are friends and nothing more." She caught her breath, counting the seconds until he replied.

When she reached five and he hadn't responded, she checked his face. The heaviness in his eyes shocked her, and her heart picked up speed. Why wasn't he agreeing with her? She had expected him to smile or even laugh, but instead, he looked...worried. He cleared his throat, interlocking his hands behind his back as he paced a step away. "I don't see any harm in it either. So long as you don't turn your constant flirtations to me instead."

Emma gasped, grateful to see a hint of amusement on his face. It was different than usual though—she could tell it was forced. "You need not worry about that," she said with a scoff. "Even if I did have some secret design on you, you have been far too absent of late." She gained the confidence to give him an accusatory look. "I have been hoping to hear your opinion of who I might pursue. You have interacted with the gentlemen during your meetings more than I have."

Harry's jaw tightened. "I'm sorry, Emma. I should not have left you to navigate this on your own."

"I don't blame you," she said in a quick voice. "I know you have been busy, as you said. The potential investments are your top concern."

He shook his head. "*You* are my top concern." That peculiar hint of color returned to his face. "I mean—it is more important that your future is comfortable than it is that I gain these investments."

Harry was quite a contradiction. A few moments before, he had acted as if he hated that she was trying to secure a husband, but now he was claiming that he wanted her to. She studied his face for a long moment before shaking herself free of her curiosity. "Have any of the men shown interest in the hotel?"

"Yes. Especially Sir Francis." The way Harry said his name—the venom behind the sound—made her pause.

"Do you not like Sir Francis?" She tipped her head to one side as she examined him further.

He seemed to have an internal debate over how to answer. "Not particularly."

"Why not?"

Harry sighed. "I should not speak ill of him. He plans to invest a great deal of money in my castle."

"I need to know what flaws in his character you have perceived. At present, he seems to be the best option for me." Emma had perceived a few flaws in him—such as his arrogance and her suspicions about his rakish tendencies. She wondered if Harry had the same thoughts.

Harry scowled. "He is *not* the best option for you."

"How do you know that?" Emma raised one eyebrow.

"He is completely absurd."

"That is very vague."

Harry covered his face with his hands, dragging his fingers down his cheeks. "I don't trust him. He said he is prepared to marry if he meets the right woman, but I worry that he is not finished being a bachelor just yet. Men like Sir Francis enjoy their freedom to..." He took a deep breath, redirecting his words. "I'm just... not certain that his intentions are honorable."

Admittedly, Emma had feared the same thing, but hearing it from Harry made her heart rear up in rebellion. "Do you think a man like Sir Francis wouldn't be happy with a woman like me?"

Harry shook his head. "Of course he would. I worry that he will break your heart, that is all."

Emma stared up at him with a scowl. There was only one person who could break her heart, and he already had. Pain swirled through her chest. "If Sir Francis is not my best option in *your* opinion, then who is?" She was just as much of a contradiction as Harry was. She had asked for his opinion, yet now that he was giving it, she was defensive.

Harry backed up and leaned against the door of the keep, watching her from a distance. "I assume you have ruled out Mr. Dudley and Lord Watlington given the head collision and the reptile obsession?"

A weak smile tugged on her mouth. "You are correct."

Harry nodded, his lips twitching before a serious expression overtook his face again. "I think Mr. Hale seems to be the most agreeable of them all."

Emma sighed. "That is the problem. Mr. Hale doesn't seem to be interested in me in the slightest. I have tried to converse with him, but he has been quite short with me. I don't envision my pursuit of him being a success at all. That is why I have been focusing my attention on Sir Francis and Mr. Seaton."

"If Mr. Seaton is still a contender, then you ought to give him more of your time. He is much better than Sir Francis." Again, Harry's jaw clenched and his nose wrinkled with distaste. He scuffed the toe of his boot at the stone ledge near the keep door.

Emma pushed down the vexation that rose in her chest. How much of Harry's dislike for Sir Francis was related to her apparent interest in him? The idea sent her mind spiraling, but she banished the thought as fast as she could. If she started to wonder if he was jealous, then her heart would concoct all sorts of ideas that weren't true. She might begin to have hope—and hope was a dangerous thing.

"Very well," she said in an offhand voice. "I suppose I should consider Mr. Seaton more carefully." That didn't mean she wouldn't still flirt with Sir Francis if Harry was nearby. The devious thought made her heart beat faster. "Will I see you at the fencing tournament this afternoon?" she asked.

Harry looked up from the ground and gave a quick nod. "I'll be there."

"I hope you'll give the gentlemen an easy competition," she said with a smile. "If you want them to like you enough to invest in your castle, you must try to keep their dignity intact. No one ever likes the person they lose to." That was why Emma wasn't very fond of Miss Fitzroy, though she had never met her.

And...Harry wasn't fond of Sir Francis.

She swallowed, putting a stop to her wayward thoughts. *He wasn't jealous.* Surely she was misinterpreting his behavior.

Harry smiled, a glint of amusement in his eyes. "You have lost to me in cards many times if I recall correctly. Does that mean you hate me?"

"Most vehemently."

His smile expanded into a grin that dented his cheek with his dimple, and Emma tried not to stare for too long. "I cannot promise that I will willingly lose to the gentlemen," he said. "It may be a good test of their characters to see how they endure a loss."

"Ah, that is a clever method of thinking. I will be watching closely."

"As will I." Harry stepped away from the keep door and returned to her side. "I'm sorry to have interrupted your walk. Are you going back inside? I'll walk with you."

Emma hesitated. "I-I probably ought to go inside alone... after my conversation with your mother, I should hate for her to think anything if she sees us together."

Harry's features protested, but he seemed to change his mind. He knew as well as she did that they couldn't risk being seen by anyone in the house at such an early hour. "You're right. I'll stay here until you're safely inside."

His warm brown eyes traced over her face until she could scarcely breathe. She glanced at his lips, and she found herself wondering for perhaps the hundredth time over the years what it might be like to kiss him. She had never kissed anyone, but she had always hoped that Harry would be the one to give her her first kiss. Her heart beat a hollow, slow rhythm, reminding her of yet another dream she wouldn't have.

Her face burned when she realized how long she had been staring so curiously at his mouth. Surely he had noticed. Her eyes darted up to his, and her heart fluttered. He wasn't giving her the confused look she had expected.

He was looking at her lips too. Her study, it seemed, had been reciprocated.

Waves of desire passed through her stomach when his eyes dragged back up to hers. In all those summers of teasing and laughing and pretending to be repulsed by the idea of kissing one another, he had never looked at her in such a way. His gaze was deeper than the sea, curious and reserved at the same time. The usual warmth she often saw in his eyes had been replaced by something new and unfamiliar. Even though she couldn't name it, she wanted to throw herself in to drown.

She took an awkward step backward, her heart in her throat. "I-I'll see you this afternoon then."

His throat shifted with a swallow, and he nodded.

The last thing she saw before turning around was his furrowed brow. She walked with hurried steps back under the gatehouse arch, his gaze burning through her back the entire way. She had intended to walk for much longer, but now that she had spent so much time speaking with Harry, she could no longer risk being seen so unpresentable. Her braided knot had already slipped halfway out, and she wasn't even wearing a proper gown under her cloak.

She slipped through the doors and toward the staircase. After she took her first step, however, a voice cut her movement short.

"Good morning, Miss Eastwood." Mrs. Coleman strode toward her from near the front window, the pleasant smile on her face fading into a frown. "Where have you been?" The silver streaks in her dark hair shone in the new sunlight streaming through the windows. She walked to the base of the staircase, stopping a few feet away.

Emma still stood on the first stair, holding tightly to the bannister as she turned around. "I went for a walk." She gave a shaky smile. Had Mrs. Coleman been watching her? How had she known she would be coming inside?

"Alone? You must know that such behavior is unacceptable."

"Yes, forgive me. I-I'm afraid I have old independent habits."

Mrs. Coleman scoffed through her nose. She walked closer until she stood on the floor just below the stair Emma stood on. "You must abide by my rules if you are to stay at this household." A warning flashed in her eyes. "*All* of them."

There was no longer any question that Mrs. Coleman had seen Emma speaking with Harry outside. How much power did Mrs. Coleman truly have? This was Harry's castle, not hers. Mrs. Coleman didn't have the power to send Emma away if Harry still welcomed her there. So why was that glint in her eyes so unsettling?

"I understand," Emma said with a nod. She smiled and turned around as quickly as she could, practically running up the stairs to escape Mrs. Coleman's watchful gaze. What was even more frightening was that Mrs. Coleman didn't try to stop her.

By the time Emma reached the top and turned around, Mrs. Coleman was gone.

Emma's heart thudded as she made her way back to her room. She should have been worried about Mrs. Coleman, but her focus was still on Harry and the hesitation on his face when she had told him about his mother's concerns.

For a moment, she had almost wondered if there was any truth to them. No. There couldn't be. If Harry had ever cared for Emma, he would have told her. He wouldn't have become engaged to someone else, no matter the reason. A wayward tear sprung up in Emma's eye, but she blinked it away. Whatever she had seen on his face—it must have been in her imagination.

CHAPTER TWELVE

E mma was the last to arrive in the great hall for the fencing tournament. She stepped through the doors, immediately greeted by the sight of five men in fencing clothes standing in various parts of the great hall. The only gentleman in the castle who was not dressed for the sport was Mr. Hale. He stood near the hearth, arms crossed, a wry smile on his mouth as he scanned the room.

A table near the largest window had been set with a variety of epees, the silver blades glistening in the sunlight. Mr. Seaton's face was also glistening as he thrust his epee forward into his imaginary opponent with a resounding grunt. His perspiring forehead wrinkled with frustration, dark curls sticking to the moisture.

Had he missed his imaginary target? That didn't quite seem possible.

The air buzzed with a competitive energy, so Emma slipped along the outskirts of the room to avoid drawing attention to herself. She recalled her conversation with

Harry about watching the match to see how each of the gentlemen behaved in a competitive environment. She had already witnessed some competitive behavior from the gentlemen—particularly Mr. Seaton and Sir Francis when it came to their attempts for her attention.

From the center of the great hall, Harry strode toward her. Her chest constricted with panic for a moment before she realized that Mrs. Coleman hadn't arrived to observe the match yet—or any interaction she had with Harry. At the moment, it was safe to speak with him.

Emma's heart rebelliously picked up speed at the sight of his disheveled chestnut hair and smiling brown eyes. His face was also glistening with perspiration, but somehow it looked far better on him than on Mr. Seaton. Since that morning, she hadn't been able to banish the image of Harry's reddened cheeks from her mind. Had she imagined it? The idea that she might have any effect on him was far more intriguing than it should have been. She had gathered from their conversation that morning that her flirting with Sir Francis had bothered him, yet that only made her want to do it more. Besides that, Harry had encouraged her to pursue Mr. Hale instead. Why did that make Mr. Hale *less* appealing? It was probably better that Harry not be involved. She would soon be doing the opposite of everything he advised her to do.

Harry stopped in front of her, catching his breath. He raked his hair back with one hand. "I'd like to hear your bets, Miss Eastwood," he said with a grin.

"Miss Eastwood?" Emma grimaced.

He gave her a knowing glance as he lowered his voice. "That is how I must refer to you here."

"Very well, *Mr. Coleman*. I'm afraid I must disappoint you. I do not make bets," she whispered with a smile. "I *cannot*—for I have not a penny to my name."

"A quandary, indeed." His dimple flashed. "But if you could place a bet, who would you expect to win today's tournament?"

A strange desire to vex him overcame her, and her answer slipped out before she could prevent it. "Sir Francis."

Harry's smile faltered a little, his brow furrowing. "Why do you say that? Has he trained as extensively as I have?"

She shrugged. "I'm not certain. He just seems like he would be proficient at everything, especially fencing." She gazed in Sir Francis's direction, even allowing a bit of false adoration to enter her eyes. Sir Francis noticed, a pompous grin instantly touching his lips. He waved. She gave a bashful smile before turning her attention back to Harry. She was performing some sort of show, hoping to get a reaction from him. She felt like a complete imp, yet she couldn't stop herself. She stole a glance at his face, noting the way his brows drew together and his smile had completely faded. Her feeling of victory only lasted a few seconds before she gave herself a thorough scolding. There was no point in making Harry feel inferior at his favorite sport. What was wrong with her?

Her heart pounded. If she wanted to be a mature lady who accepted her losses gracefully, then she needed to banish any spite she felt toward Harry's decision to marry Miss Fitzroy. He hadn't given *Emma* any expectation or indication that he would marry her one day. The only expectation that had entered her heart had been of her own making.

Harry didn't deserve her spite, but somehow it was bandaging the wounds on her heart to see the signs of jealousy in him, even if they were only in her mind.

Just when she was about to change her bet, Harry took a step back, a determined look on his face. "Well, we shall see if Sir Francis is as *proficient* as you think he is." He smiled, but his voice ran thick with irritation. "In the meantime, you ought to go speak with Mr. Hale. He isn't participating in the tournament and is alone by the hearth. You would be wise to take the opportunity to further your acquaintance with him." Without another word, he turned around and joined the men at the center of the room again.

Emma's face burned, a wave of anger assailing her chest. What had Sir Francis even done to earn Harry's dislike? And what was so angelic about Mr. Hale that made Harry recommend him? All Mr. Hale had done was act aloof toward her. In fact, she was quite intimidated by him. She pressed down her anger for long enough to glance at the hearth where Mr. Hale stood, leaning against one side of it with his arms folded. He likely hadn't even spared a glance in her direction since she had entered the great hall.

Her chest still spiraled with frustration, but she couldn't deny that Harry was right. She would be foolish to watch the tournament alone when she had such an obvious opportunity in front of her. Mr. Hale was the only man among the party who she hardly knew, yet he seemed to be the most well-mannered—if not a little unapproachable.

She squared her shoulders as she walked toward him. His eyes finally shifted in her direction when she was a few feet away.

"Good afternoon, Mr. Hale." Emma smiled, and he gave a polite bow in greeting.

"Miss Eastwood." The cordial smile on his lips only lasted a brief moment before he was stoic again. His dark auburn hair was cut neatly over the tops of his ears, and the front was combed away from his forehead, giving her a clear view of his striking green eyes and the subtle smattering of freckles across his nose and cheekbones. He was certainly handsome, but in a different way than Sir Francis. It was a more...humble sort of handsome—the same sort of handsome that Harry was.

She stopped her thoughts from making any more comparisons.

"Are you not fond of fencing?" she asked with a nod toward the other men.

Mr. Hale's eyes shifted toward her, but his head didn't move. "I prefer to watch rather than participate."

"Is it because you haven't been trained?" she asked in a curious voice.

He seemed surprised by the pointed question, and perhaps it had been too bold. "I *have* been trained. My training was quite thorough. I was taught at Angelo's Fencing Academy in London."

"Then why not go claim your victory over all of these men?" she asked, throwing him a teasing glance. "I would argue that there are at least a few egos in need of diminishing." Her gaze traveled to Harry first, who happened to be observing her conversation with Mr. Hale while he tested the weight of his epee. She lifted her chin as she gave her full attention to Mr. Hale again. Would Harry suddenly dislike him too if she was seen flirting with him?

Mr. Hale sighed as he turned to face her. "Fencing is all sport and entertainment during a tournament like this, but it is not always so innocent. Having seen the darker side of such an activity, I cannot find enjoyment in it." A sad smile touched his lips before his eyes shifted away from her again. It seemed to be his way of ending the conversation.

Well that was certainly cryptic.

Emma studied the side of his face, but he remained completely unfazed by her attention. At this rate, she may have to eliminate him simply because he wasn't interested in her. Could his mind be changed in the short weeks that remained of the house party? It was doubtful. Her heart sank. That meant Sir Francis and Mr. Seaton were still her best options.

She turned her gaze to the center of the great hall, where the first two opponents were beginning their bout. It was Mr. Dudley against Sir Francis. Mr. Dudley's brow was sweating and glistening, which accentuated his bruise. The fear in his eyes was obvious as Sir Francis took his first step toward him. In a panic, Mr. Dudley thrust his blade forward, but Sir Francis avoided it with a counter-parry. Emma watched with growing embarrassment for poor Mr. Dudley. It took only a few minutes for Sir Francis to score five touches against him with ease.

It seemed she was right. Sir Francis was proficient at fencing. She exchanged a glance with Harry. His jaw was tight, his eyes fixed on Sir Francis.

The bouts carried on with various partnerships, and Emma found herself amazed at Harry's skill. She had watched him fence only once, several years before, and his skill had improved a great deal since. There was something about his demeanor when he was engaged in sport that made her heart skip. He smiled at times, his dimple flashing, but when he was focused and serious, he was equally attractive. She should have been focusing on the other men, but she was allowing Harry to distract her yet again. Mr. Hale remained silent beside her, his eyes narrowed with concentration as he observed each bout. When Harry scored his last point on Mr. Seaton, an alarming scream rang through the great hall.

Emma jumped.

Mr. Seaton threw his epee to the floor, creating a resounding clatter. He stormed across the room, face red and dripping with perspiration. He swigged angrily at his cup of water, eyes ablaze.

Against her will, her gaze darted to Harry. His lips quivered, and she had to fight to hide her own smile. The aftermath of Mr. Seaton's reaction hung in the air as all the men watched him in stunned silence as he drained every last drop from his glass of water before slamming it down on the table in frustration.

Any interest Emma might have had in him scattered like leaves in a storm. She could not tolerate such an unpredictable temperament. If he couldn't manage his own temper, how could he be trusted to treat her with kindness and respect? This was a friendly fencing match, not a matter of life and death.

His reaction was completely ridiculous. His face was shinier and redder than a bowl of fresh raspberry jam.

"Here is yet another reason I did not wish to participate." The voice belonged to Mr. Hale. Emma was so shocked to hear him speak to her willingly that it took her a moment to recognize that he was addressing her.

She glanced up at his face. He was watching Mr. Seaton's behavior with a grimace.

"To Mr. Seaton's credit, it shows how much he cares for the sport," Emma said. "It must matter a great deal to him if he is so upset to be losing."

A hint of a smile washed across his face. "I suppose that is true."

While Mr. Seaton struggled to calm his temper, Harry and Sir Francis prepared for their bout, the one that would determine the champion. Sir Francis smiled, a taunting grin that Emma already knew would vex Harry to no end. Harry's expression was calculating and serious, but Sir Francis did not appear intimidated in the slightest. With his other opponents, Harry had been smiling and even laughing.

Not anymore.

The room was silent until Sir Francis spoke to Harry. "Did you mention what the winner of this tournament would receive? Is there some sort of prize?"

Harry's seriousness broke for a brief moment, a smile tugging his mouth upward. "I don't believe I mentioned one."

"How can we have a tournament with no prize for the winner? Where is the motivation in that?"

Harry's brow lifted. "Are you expecting to win?"

Sir Francis smiled, one eyebrow cocking upward. "Well... I should not say. It is not good practice to offend my host."

The other men in the room chuckled. Emma watched the growing look of contemplation on Harry's face. "Name your prize. If you win, you shall be granted it. If I win, I shall be granted the same."

Sir Francis's eyes drifted in Emma's direction. "I should like to win the opportunity to spend an entire afternoon with Miss Eastwood."

Emma felt a wave of heat rise to her cheeks as all eyes in the room drifted to her—including Harry's.

His gaze lingered on her for several seconds. "That is not mine to offer," Harry said. "Such terms can only be set if Miss Eastwood agrees to them."

Emma's heart picked up speed. What if Harry won? How would Mrs. Coleman react if she knew he would be spending an afternoon with her? She reminded herself that Sir Francis hadn't specified that it was a courtship outing or anything romantic, so she and Harry could simply ride horses, or better yet, abandon his 'prize' altogether.

Emma cleared her throat, but when she spoke, it still began as a squeak. "Y-yes. I'll agree to it."

Sir Francis threw her a flirtatious smile.

Harry's brow furrowed in concentration as the bout began. Emma nearly began chewing her fingernail, a habit she had long abandoned. She felt the tension like a rope around her ribs, her lungs hardly able to expand as she watched the two men competing. After matching one another's points for several minutes, Sir Francis took the final point, ending the bout as the winner.

Harry grunted and stepped away, his hair wet with perspiration. He took a deep breath, his mouth a grim line. He was obviously upset by the loss, but he had held his composure far better than Mr. Seaton had. Emma's heart sank as she watched the growing look of defeat on Harry's face. He flashed a smile and clapped Sir Francis on the shoulder, congratulating him before turning around. Emma could no longer see his face, but she found herself craning her neck in an attempt to sneak a view of his profile.

"Oh, dear," Emma muttered to herself. She glanced up at Mr. Hale, who was also observing Harry's reaction. "This is quite uncharacteristic of him. He isn't usually so upset by friendly matches. Perhaps Mr. Seaton's temper has influenced him for the worse." She laughed, but it sounded hollow.

Mr. Hale shrugged. "Or perhaps it's because what he is losing matters a great deal to him."

His words sank in slowly, one at a time. "Losing?"

"An afternoon spent with you."

Emma shook her head fast. They had spent countless afternoons together at Stansham playing cards, reading books, riding horses. The only thing Harry was disappointed to lose was his pride. "Harry doesn't care to spend an afternoon with *me*."

Mr. Hale gave a knowing smile that made her heart race. "Harry?"

Drat. She had used his Christian name. "Yes, Harry. He and I have been friends since we were children. That is the only reason for my informal address."

Mr. Hale gave a slow nod. "I see." His eyes shifted in her direction. "But that does not change the fact that he wanted to spend an afternoon with you."

Emma needed to clear up this misinterpretation at once. She couldn't tell him Harry was engaged, so she searched for some other reason. "I'm certain you are mistaken, Mr. Hale," Emma said in a confident voice. "Mr. Coleman has far too much to do than to spend so much time with me. He has been quite busy since inheriting Garsley."

Mr. Hale was silent for a long moment, his features reflecting deep thought. He said nothing more on the subject, which only made her more nervous.

After Mr. Seaton's tantrum, she could no longer view him in a positive light. That left only Sir Francis or Mr. Hale. Even though he didn't seem interested, Emma still couldn't risk Mr. Hale believing that there was something between her and Harry.

Perhaps it was too late. Did she have to eliminate him too?

Sir Francis walked toward her with a grin, his blond hair disheveled on his forehead. He could very well be her only remaining option, so she put a broad smile on her face. "Congratulations on your win, sir."

He raked his hair back with one hand, his eyes raking in a similar manner over her face. "I thank you for offering such a tempting prize."

Well, it hadn't been Emma who offered it. It had been entirely his idea. From over Sir Francis's shoulder, she saw Harry watching their conversation. He was drinking a glass of water, but that did little to hide his perturbation. He turned away when she noticed him, but she suspected he was still listening.

"How could I not agree to the prospect of spending an afternoon with you?" Emma said in a loud voice. "I'm certain it will be an enjoyable time."

Sir Francis grinned, and she shifted uncomfortably. How long would she have to put on an act around him? He was handsome, but she was not drawn to him as she pretended to be. She hated to agree with Harry, but there was something in his character that bothered her. It could have been his arrogance or how he simply made her feel uneasy instead of safe and warm like she would have hoped for.

As Sir Francis walked away, he leaned close with a whisper. "I look forward to it."

CHAPTER THIRTEEN

It didn't matter where he was—the home he had been raised in, Stansham, or Garsley—the library had always been Harry's sanctuary. It was where he went to think, to relax, to brood—whatever it was. At the moment, he was feeling rather broody, and that wasn't common for him. His emotions were boiling like a stew inside his chest, each ingredient sour and bitter.

He was finally prepared to face them.

He sank down in his leather chair, leaning his head back and closing his eyes. His hands curled into fists on the arms of his chair. Practically since the first moment Emma had arrived at Garsley he hadn't been able to stop thinking of her. He had expended so much energy trying not to allow her to swallow his thoughts, but he had lost the fight day after day.

All these years, Emma had been his friend. He had thought of her often and looked forward to seeing her each year, but he had never dared to hope or expect that she could be anything more to him than that—a friend. His confidant. His opponent in cards. He couldn't deny that the thought had crossed his mind of what it might be like to marry her one day. It had made him happy to think of, but also hopeless.

He didn't like being out of control.

Any dreams he had—inheriting Garsley, traveling the continent one day, starting his hotel—were all within his control. They were guaranteed either by his uncle's written will or by Harry's own ambition and hard work. He had been terrified to think of proposing to Emma one day, only because he could not guarantee her answer. It wasn't in his control. He hadn't been able to decipher whether she cared for him as more than a friend, and he had been too cowardly to ask.

He had been too afraid to lose, so he hadn't even tried.

His throat tightened as the realization melted over him. If he had always liked to be in control of himself and his emotions, why had he allowed himself to be controlled by fear? Had he supposed that he would be content watching Emma marry someone else? He had buried his dream of spending his life with her beneath other things, especially his dream of the hotel. When he had met Miss Fitzroy, she was a safe escape. She was calm and serious and she didn't make him feel things he didn't understand. She shared his ambition and she had been a welcome distraction. The hotel had become his focus, and for a moment, he had been foolish enough to believe that he could be happy without Emma.

But now he knew that it wasn't true. He was in love with her.

He always had been.

His heart had buried the dream of her, but recent events had been digging it out, revealing just how raw Harry's feelings truly were. Imagining Emma with any other man was torturous, yet there was nothing Harry could do to stop it. He had made a promise to Miss Fitzroy, and his honor demanded that he keep it. Her reputation required that he keep it. All he could do now was sit back and endure the pain of seeing Emma courted by these other men and wonder—what if he had courted her first? What if he hadn't been engaged when she had arrived at Garsley? Did she feel anything—even the slightest *something*—for him?

He shushed his thoughts. Even if she did, it didn't matter. Anything they could have had was over before it had begun.

Regret swirled around his heart as he tried to calm his breathing. He had bathed and changed into clean clothes after the fencing tournament, but he felt like his body hadn't relaxed. He was still defensive and tense. How had he lost to Sir Francis? His jaw tightened. He had lost in more ways than one.

The door to the library creaked, but he couldn't see it from where his chair was tucked in the corner. He sat up straighter, listening to the rustling footsteps. There were only two people in the house whose footsteps would *rustle* against what must have been skirts. Mother or Emma. His heart pounded, and he decided to guess the first option.

"Mother?"

The rustling stopped for a moment, then resumed. "Guess again."

It was Emma's voice.

Despite all the worry and pain inside him, her words still brought a smile to his face. "Hmm," he mused. "Is it Mr. Seaton?"

Emma's face peeked around one of the bookshelves with a hesitant smile. She clutched a book to her chest. "I shall take great offense to that. I didn't think my voice sounded so angry."

"Or extremely masculine?" Harry raised a brow.

Emma laughed, her lashes fluttering down toward the floor. "I'm glad to know you find Mr. Seaton 'extremely masculine.' I shall take that opinion into account."

Harry laughed. Emma was far from masculine. Her voice was high and soft, musical even when she wasn't singing. "I didn't know you cared for my opinion," he said.

As Emma strode around the corner with her book, he offered her the chair beside him. Her brow furrowed as she sat down. "What do you mean?"

Harry should not have been speaking his mind, but he couldn't help it. "I advised you against pursuing Sir Francis, yet you don't seem to have taken that into account." He tried to keep his voice lighthearted, but she didn't seem to interpret it that way.

The crease in her brow deepened. "I don't entirely understand your aversion to him. He is a willing investor for your hotel. I thought that detail alone would endear him to you." There was an edge of bitterness in her voice that surprised him.

"An interest in my hotel isn't enough to make me like him," Harry said with a laugh.

"Was it not enough to make you like Miss Fitzroy?" Emma asked in a quiet voice.

Harry's heart thudded. "That is different."

"How so?" Emma leaned forward, her curious eyes never leaving his face. She looked nervous, but she wore a mask of confidence.

Harry shifted uncomfortably, his throat suddenly raw and at a loss for words. "Miss Fitzroy and I became engaged as a business agreement. It wasn't a matter of *liking* her."

"Why does my husband need to be likable then?" Emma asked. "My marriage could also feel like a cold business agreement."

Harry leaned closer to her on his chair. "But Sir Francis does not stand to gain anything by marrying you. That is what makes me nervous. A man like him doesn't seem keen to give up his life as a bachelor."

Emma's eyes fell. "Of course. I am worthless to a man if I don't have money."

Harry sighed. Why could he not phrase things correctly? "That's not what I meant. You have much to offer that is of far greater worth than money. I'm certain you would make him very happy indeed. You are good, kind, witty, talented and...beautiful." Her gaze flickered to his face, her blue eyes cautious and heavy. It tugged at his heart. He swallowed, gathering his thoughts again. "I don't trust Sir Francis to recognize that as he should. He is too...*daft*." But still not as daft as Harry had been.

Emma's eyes flashed with anger. "You don't know that. At present, he is the only man who has paid me constant attention. After today, I have to eliminate Mr. Seaton for his temper, and I tried to converse with Mr. Hale but he seems even more opposed to my company with each attempt." She lifted her chin. "You must understand why I continue to pursue Sir Francis."

"I still don't think it is wise," Harry said.

Emma's determination only seemed to grow. "I am not free to be wise. Even if Mr. Hale is the best option, he will not be convinced to court me." She paused. "Unless you speak to him and encourage such a thing."

Nothing sounded worse to Harry than trying to persuade a man to court Emma. But how selfish would he be to refuse? The truth of the matter was that he was not in a position to marry her himself, no matter how much he regretted that. If he truly cared for Emma, he would be doing all he could to ensure she was engaged by the end of the house party. As opposed as he was to Sir Francis, he needed to do something to help her secure the attention of Mr. Hale instead.

"Very well," Harry said with a weak smile. "I will speak to Mr. Hale."

Emma sat back in surprise. "Really? What will you say to him?"

"I'll tell him how wonderful you are." His voice was quiet. A stream of sunlight from the window cast a line across Emma's face as she looked up at him. "I'll tell him he would be a fool not to take his chance to come to know you, and that if he is in a position to marry you, he would be the happiest of men." Emotion threaded through his voice, and he didn't even try to hide it. He held her gaze, his heart beating a wild rhythm.

Emma looked down at her book, fiddling with the bent corner of the cover. Color bled onto her cheeks. What would he give to touch her face? The urge was so sudden, so poignant, that Harry could hardly breathe.

"You don't need to say *all* of that." She peeked at him. "He will think that I sent you to say such things."

"I'll ensure he knows that it is all my own opinion, and that it is entirely true." His throat was dry as he studied her downcast eyes. "Every word."

"I...I wish that you had won the fencing match today," Emma said. She brushed a blonde ringlet from her forehead as she sat up straighter. "I would have much preferred to spend an afternoon with you. All this courting is quite exhausting."

Harry's heart lifted at her words. "Well, Sir Francis did not claim *this* afternoon, did he? You might stay here in the library with me a little longer."

Emma's eyes flooded with reservation, the corners drooping with sadness. "But you *did* lose the match." She stood in one swift motion. "So I must go."

He laughed, but his chest ached at the same time. "What might I do to win more of your time? It did not always cost so much to sit with you in the library for an afternoon."

She turned around, holding the book tightly. "I don't think Miss Fitzroy, if she were here, would be pleased if I stayed. And given your engagement, your mother has also been quite direct with me on her wishes that I stay away from you. Our circumstances are not—they cannot—be the same as they were." She took a deep breath. "I think you would agree."

Harry didn't want to agree, but he knew that she was right. He gave a swift nod. The pain rising inside of him felt like a blow to the chest. "You're right. I will not keep you here any longer."

Her eyes captured his for a long moment as she backed away. His heart ached when she finally turned around.

"Good day, Harry."

"Wait, Emma." He stood abruptly.

Her eyes were wide when she turned to him again. "Yes?"

"I wish to be of assistance in any way I can in your quest for a husband." He tightened his jaw. "I have not been very helpful, and I'm sorry. But I hope that from now on you will trust me with any part of the task."

She eyed him carefully. "Even if I choose Sir Francis?"

"Even then." Harry looked down at the floor. "All I want is for you to be happy and well cared for. If Sir Francis can and will make you happy, then I have nothing against him."

She gave a slow nod. "I want you to be happy as well." She took a deep breath and flashed a smile. A hint of color still remained on her cheeks. "It is my hope that Miss Fitzroy and your hotel will make you so." Was her voice shaking?

Harry had never felt more empty. "Thank you." The happiness that he hoped to obtain from the hotel and his marriage to Miss Fitzroy felt like a shadow compared to the happiness he would feel if Emma were living constantly within the walls of Garsley. Ambition could never fill his heart the way love could. But that realization had come far too late.

Her eyes turned to liquid, but before he could stop her, she turned the corner around the bookcase. He listened to the door close behind her, and the finality of it drove a dagger through his heart. He stared at the back of the book-case until his vision went out of focus.

Would it be better or worse to know if she loved him too?

That question would haunt him the most.

CHAPTER FOURTEEN

Mrs. Coleman was unavailable to chaperone for Emma's afternoon outing with Sir Francis, so she sent Isabel in her place. Part of Emma was relieved that Mrs. Coleman wouldn't be watching her every move, but the maid might not be quite as attentive as Emma would have liked. For once she wished for Mrs. Coleman's observant nature, if only to ensure Sir Francis remained the gentleman she hoped he was.

He was wealthy, handsome, and very attentive toward her. He was confident—bordering on arrogant, to be sure—but if she was going to remain positive, then confident was a better word to use. If he truly had marriage in mind, then what more could she ask for in a husband, at least among the five bachelors in attendance?

She couldn't give him any reason to change his opinion of her. That afternoon was imperative to her success; she could sense it as she tugged her new gloves over her fingers. Every single article of clothing she now owned was a gift from Harry—a gift meant to make her presentable and help her secure a husband. She could not ruin this opportunity.

Her thoughts drifted back to her conversation with Harry the day before in the library. She hadn't been able to forget his words, the ones he planned to relay to Mr. Hale. *I'll tell him he would be a fool not to take his chance to come to know you, and that if he is in a position to marry you, he would be the happiest of men.*

Emma rubbed a circle over her chest, taking a shaky breath. Were those words honest? If Harry truly believed that, then why hadn't he married her himself?

She might have been losing her mind—or perhaps she was burdened with too many glimpses of hope—but there were moments when she wondered if Harry regretted his choice to marry Miss Fitzroy. What would she give to know the answer? Even though he was a man of honor who would never break off the engagement, if she *knew* that he regretted it, she would feel better.

She chewed her lip.

Or perhaps she would only feel worse. Regret could not change the past.

She redirected her distracted thoughts to Sir Francis. She was about to meet him out in the garden. He had arranged a picnic, and her stomach fluttered with nervousness. She had interacted with him many times with the entire group present, but never alone with only a maid as her chaperone. Their conversation would have to be more prolonged, and she would have to prove her intelligence and wit in ways that she hadn't been able to prove to Mr. Hale. She couldn't allow any thoughts of Harry to distract her.

Emma straightened the edge of her spencer jacket,

taking a deep breath as Isabel followed her outside to the courtyard. Sir Francis was already standing at the center, holding a picnic basket on one arm and a blanket on the other. Emma wiped the nervous expression from her face, putting on a polite smile instead.

"Miss Eastwood," Sir Francis said with a bow. His gaze traveled across her figure and back to her face again. Her stomach turned, but she pretended she hadn't noticed his extensive study of her approach. His broad shoulders pulled tight against his jacket as his posture straightened.

"Good afternoon, Sir Francis." She clasped her hands together in front of her.

He extended his arm for her to take as they started walking. Warm sunlight filtered through the thin clouds, illuminating pale lines in his blue irises. The intensity of his gaze was rather shocking, so she focused on the grass ahead.

He was leading her toward the nearby trees, which only intensified her nerves. "Where are we going?" she asked.

"There is a clearing in the woods that is especially peaceful." Sir Francis gave her a reassuring smile. "I thought you might like it."

"Ah." Emma gulped, turning around to see if Isabel was still trailing behind her. She had fully expected to see the girl with her apron and straight dark hair, but there was no one else in sight. Where on earth had she gone? Emma stopped walking, turning around fully. "My maid—" she frowned. "Did you see where she went?"

Sir Francis raised his brows innocently. "I didn't. How strange." He continued walking, offering his arm to Emma again.

She hesitated. "I shouldn't be without a chaperone." A nervous laugh escaped her.

"Where is your sense of adventure, Miss Eastwood?" he challenged.

She couldn't seem boring or strict, could she? That would hardly induce him to marry her. She gave a demure smile and walked faster, following him to the clearing he had told her about. He set out the picnic blanket, placing the basket on one of the corners. Then he sat down, patting the space beside him.

Why was she so nervous? Isabel had vanished, and she was alone in the woods with a notorious flirt. Harry's warnings rang through her head, but she pushed them away as she joined Sir Francis on the blanket.

He tipped his head down to look into her eyes, moving closer to her. "This is actually quite opportune. I have been hoping to find a moment alone with you."

Her heart raced. Had she already done enough to convince him to propose? Her stomach roiled with a mixture of relief and terror. How could she accept his proposal when her heart was so entirely uninvolved? She had known she would likely be marrying a man she didn't love if she chose to stay and seek a husband from the guests at Garsley. That reality hadn't fully struck her until that moment.

She felt ill, but she gave him an encouraging smile. "With so many other guests at Garsley I'm certain it was no small task."

"What you must know about me, Miss Eastwood, is that I do not give up when there is something that I want." He leaned toward her on the picnic blanket and caught a loose strand of her hair between his fingers, tucking it behind her ear.

Good heavens, he was so close.

She didn't like it.

Her heart picked up speed. She started to lean away. Before she could, his hand slid behind her neck, and he brought her face closer. She hardly had time to react before he pressed his mouth to hers. The shock of the kiss took a few seconds to sink in, but by then, his arms were wrapped all the way around her. She had often dreamed of her first kiss and how it might feel. She had imagined that she might feel lightheaded or elated, with a fluttering in her stomach or heart, but at the moment, all she could feel were two wet lips.

And an overwhelming sense of panic.

Sir Francis was pressing toward her with surprising strength, and she finally managed to pull her face away from his.

Her cheeks burned. "Sir Francis—" she shook her head, struggling to find the words. "I should find my chaperone." She hoped that would be hint enough that she didn't wish to continue kissing him, but he either didn't listen or didn't care.

He laughed. "I thought you would be happy to be rid of her." Without giving Emma a chance to protest, he kissed her again, this time with enough force to make her tip over onto the picnic blanket. The weight of his chest covered hers as his cold lips kissed her mouth without any return of the affection. "Stop," she managed to demand between his uninvited kisses.

He didn't stop.

Anger surged inside her, mingling with enough fear to give her a burst of strength. She pushed hard against his shoulders, and when that did little to dissuade him, she jerked her knee upward.

He grunted, rolling off of her in one swift motion.

She hurried to her feet, her heart racing. Now she might truly be ill. Her unsettled stomach turned at the realization of what had just happened. She glared at him, catching her breath as she watched him roll in pain on the ground. The hateful cad! When he had expressed his gratitude to have a moment alone with her, she had hoped he meant that it was an opportunity to propose. How naive could she be? How pathetically trusting? Harry had warned her, but she hadn't listened. Her eyes burned with sudden tears.

Sir Francis's brow contracted, a dark expression on his face. As he started to stand, Emma turned around, running as quickly as she could over the grass until she was out of the cover of the trees. She didn't stop running until she was inside the castle. The door slammed shut behind her, echoing in the dim space.

A lump formed in her throat, and she wiped at her lips with disgust. How revolting. She had hoped that kissing would be enjoyable, but that...*that* was far from it. Tears sprung to her eyes, but she blinked them away as fast as she could. She sniffed and made a retching sound that was far too loud in the vast entryway.

Her tears escaped, falling down her cheeks. She pressed a hand to her chest, struggling to catch her breath as she kept her eyes fixed on the door. What if he caught up to her? She was safe in Garsley, wasn't she?

The sound of hurried footsteps in the corridor behind her made her jump. "Emma?"

She whirled around, her heart beating impossibly faster. Harry strode toward her, his features flooding with concern. He held a paper with an architectural drawing in one hand, as if he had rushed out of his study so quickly he had forgotten to leave it behind. At the sight of his face, her tears began falling freely. She cowered near the wall and looked down at the rug beneath her feet. How embarrassing would it be to admit to him what had happened?

Harry rushed forward, taking her shoulders softly between his hands. "Are you hurt?" He searched her face, his eyes frantic and worried.

She shook her head. "No," she squeaked.

"What happened?" He wiped at a tear that hung from her jaw, then at another on her cheek. She stared up at him, perplexed by the warmth that each of his touches sent spiraling over her skin. Her body relaxed, her fear vanishing instantly. Even so, the tears still fell, and she realized that her legs were shaking.

Emma closed her eyes, her face burning all over again. How could she tell him what had happened? She took a shaky breath. If she told Harry, would he insist that Sir Francis marry her? Would he hold him to his honor? The thought was terrifying.

Before she could begin, the door opened behind her, making her jump closer to Harry. She glanced slowly behind her shoulder. Sir Francis stood in the doorway, and when he took in the scene, his angry expression smoothed over.

He gave a casual smile. "Ah, Mr. Coleman." He cleared his throat, striding forward with a slight grimace. Good. He was still in pain. "I hope Miss Eastwood has not... exaggerated any of the details of our outing. Unfortunately this is not the first time a woman has tried to ensnare me. I think it is best that we keep all of this quiet."

Emma sensed Harry's muscles stiffen, and when she looked up at his face, his eyes were hard, his jaw tight as he stared at Sir Francis. "Keep *what* quiet, exactly?"

Sir Francis's smile twitched. "Well—er—Miss Eastwood's attempts to seduce me were quite inappropriate, but we need not dwell on them any longer."

Emma shook her head, glaring at him. "That is not true."

Harry stepped forward, addressing Sir Francis with an unyielding voice. "I require all the details of your outing. Now. Miss Eastwood is under my protection here, and if you have done anything to harm her—"

"Harm?" Sir Francis chuckled. "No harm has been done, I assure you."

Even though hot anger burned in Emma's veins, she was frozen. She composed her fear enough to speak. "He kissed me," she said in a raspy voice. She didn't dare look at Harry or Sir Francis, so she stared at her hands instead, wringing them together. She gulped as her face burned all over again. "Repeatedly, and against my wishes. I managed to stop him and then immediately ran inside."

Silence fell, and it was deafening. Sir Francis wasn't denying it.

Finally, she heard Harry's deep inhale. "I will give you one hour to pack your trunk and be out of sight of Garsley." His voice shook with suppressed anger. "You are never welcome to set foot here again, or anywhere near Miss Eastwood."

Sir Francis scoffed with disbelief. "You won't have any of my investment."

"And you won't have any of the profits."

Emma carefully stole a glance at Harry's face. She had never seen him so angry. Her heart pounded with dread.

"Why are you still standing there?" Harry barked. "If you have no intention of offering a proposal to Miss Eastwood, then there is no reason you should still be burdening her with the task of looking upon you a moment longer."

Sir Francis gave a quiet laugh, shaking his head. "I have far too much sense to propose to a woman with no money or family."

Emma's stomach dropped, his words pinching her heart. She squared her shoulders. "You have more sense than honor, it would seem. Thankfully I have far too much sense to accept you even if you did propose."

Sir Francis smirked. "I'm glad we are in agreement." He gave an exaggerated bow before striding past them in the direction of the staircase beyond the vestibule.

Harry took a deep breath as he passed. His restraint from throwing a facer at Sir Francis seemed to be hanging by a thread.

As Sir Francis walked by, he paused, leaning toward Harry with a rankling smirk. "I confess it surprised me that a woman of Miss Eastwood's breeding didn't know how to kiss. Perhaps if she had been more practiced, we would still be in the woods right now and you would be unaware." His words were obviously meant to provoke Harry, and it worked.

Harry's mouth was a firm line as he threw his fist at Sir Francis's face, making solid contact with his nose. Sir Francis threw his head back in pain for a brief moment before a snarl escaped his throat and he lunged at Harry, shoving his chest with both hands. He swung at Harry's face, striking his cheekbone.

Emma jumped back. "Stop! Both of you!"

Harry grabbed Sir Francis by the front of his shirt, throwing him back several paces. Sir Francis stumbled, barely managing to keep his balance. He wiped the trickle of blood under his nose, and when he bared his teeth in an unsettling smile, they were also covered in blood. "I'll take my leave as you asked," he spat. "You may have Miss Eastwood—and the failure of your business venture—all to yourself." He gave another of his mocking bows before continuing out of the room with his hand held against his nose.

As soon as his footfalls had faded, Emma's emotions unraveled a second time. She rushed toward Harry, who was touching his cheekbone gingerly.

"Are you all right?" she asked in a worried voice.

His eyes were still ablaze, but the moment they settled on her, they melted. "You should not be concerned about me. Are *you* all right?"

She swallowed the lump in her throat. "Yes," she choked. "But his investment—it is all my fault you have lost it." She exhaled as a tear fell down her cheek. "I knew he was a cad. *I knew it*, but I hoped I was wrong." She squeezed her eyes shut for a moment before looking up at Harry. "I'm so sorry. And now you're hurt."

"I'm not hurt as badly as Sir Francis. Or as badly as you.

He deserved far worse than a bruised nose for taking advantage of you in such a way." His brow contracted with anger as his eyes fell to Emma's lips. Were they permanently stained now with Sir Francis's revolting kisses? Her heart ached. What must Harry have thought of her? He had seen her flirting with him.

Without thinking, she lifted her fingers to Harry's face, brushing them softly over the swelling red skin on his cheekbone. She traced the perimeter of the bruise, then swiped her fingers across the middle. She felt his eyes locked on her face as she went, but she didn't dare look at them. "This is what my mother used to do when I had a wound," she said in a hoarse voice. "She traced her fingers across my injury, and when she finished, she said she had *erased it.*" Emma laughed. "Somehow I believed her. The pain always seemed to go away after that. So not to worry. I erased it."

Harry's eyes were heavy as they bored into hers. She awkwardly lowered her hand.

To her surprise, Harry pulled her into his arms. Her breath hitched as his arms wrapped around her back, her head falling into place against his chest. Her body was enveloped in warmth, and her legs stopped shaking. Somehow his closeness made her emotions spiral even further out of her control, but as she listened to his heartbeat in the silence, she knew why. Being held by Harry like that—it was the first and last time.

She sniffed, struggling to remain calm amid the turmoil inside her. "I'm sorry you lost Sir Francis's investment. It's my fault for pursuing him when you warned me against it."

She felt his next inhale before he spoke again. "I *don't care* about his investment. Your comfort and safety is far more important to me." She felt his chin rest on top of her head, and his next words rustled against her hair. "*You* are far more important to me."

Emma closed her eyes as one last tear soaked into Harry's shirt. She would do well not to take his words to mean more than they did. The truth of the matter was that he had her heart—he always had—but she couldn't allow him to keep it. Somehow she had to learn to get it back, to give it to someone else. The longer he held her, the more impossible that seemed.

She leaned back to look up at his face. His arms loosened, but only a little. Her heart raced at the closeness of his face to hers—his warm brown eyes running over her like a peaceful summer stream. "I'm sorry I lost the fencing match to Sir Francis," he muttered. "I could have prevented you being in that situation if I were better skilled at fencing."

Emma laughed, but it was breathless. "I would have much rather spent an afternoon with you." A surge of wistful longing swirled in her chest as Harry's eyes locked with hers, a smile transforming them. That dimple appeared in his cheek. Her words continued to spill out. "If you had won, I could have spent the afternoon playing cards and reading books and *not* being kissed." She grimaced at the recent memory of Sir Francis's advances. "I never knew kissing was so...disagreeable." She regretted her confession the moment it escaped, but she had needed to confide her disappointment in *someone.* Perhaps it shouldn't have been Harry, but it was too late. He was already staring at her with a furrowed brow.

Her cheeks grew hot at his study of her face. "Don't be surprised that I was so inexperienced with kissing," she said. "I had never kissed a man before and I hated every moment of it." She never would have discussed such a subject with any man but Harry.

A wry smile crossed his features.

"Don't laugh at me!" She looked down at his cravat, taking a deep breath. He was still holding her so close. Did he realize that? Or had he forgotten that his hands were still around her waist? How could he forget such a detail when it was practically all she could think of?

"I'm not laughing at you," Harry said in a serious voice.

"Then why are you smiling?" She raised an eyebrow.

Harry bit his lower lip, shaking his head.

She pushed her hand against his chest teasingly. "Why?"

That smile she had accused him of was gone, and she wondered if it had anything to do with how she had touched him. He took a deep breath. "It is unfair that your first kiss was stolen in such a way. But...part of me is glad to hear that you aren't swooning."

Emma met his gaze, her heart quickening. What did he mean by that?

"Because I never liked Sir Francis," he added too quickly.

"You made that very obvious." Emma tried to smile, but her entire body was weak. All she could feel was Harry's closeness, his hands and arms and the weight of his gaze. "I like him much less now that I've found how rakish he is. And how horrible it felt to kiss him." She shuddered.

Harry laughed softly. "Do not be so disheartened. You won't always hate kissing."

Emma scowled. "How do you know I won't?"

"With the right man, you will find it to be all you've dreamed of." Harry's soft brown eyes lowered momentarily to her lips, but it was so quick, she wondered if she had imagined it. His hair fell over his brow, and she was tempted to brush it away for him. Blast it all, she was tempted to do much more than that. After such a horrific experience being kissed by Sir Francis, how was it that she still wanted to be kissed by Harry?

"I wish I could forget it ever happened," she said.

Harry's eyes searched hers for a few seconds, a curious look in them. And then his brow furrowed in concentration as his hand lifted to her face. She froze, her heart skittering as his thumb brushed against the edge of her mouth. She stared at his downcast lashes as his concentrated gaze followed his thumb over the length of her lower lip, and then across the top one. A shiver followed the touch, racing down her neck and shoulder blades. His throat bobbed with a swallow, and his eyes found hers again. "Not to worry. I erased it."

Emma could hardly move. Or breathe. She wanted to laugh, or smile at the very least, but he had rendered her useless. His fingertips grazed her cheek before falling away.

The sound of heavy footfalls made her jump, and she quickly took a step back. Mr. Hale had walked into the vestibule. His brows lifted in surprise at her abrupt movement.

"Mr. Hale," she greeted, her voice shaky. Were her emotions still playing out on her face?

"Miss Eastwood," he returned. His attention drifted to Harry, a curious look on his face. Emma's heart sank. Mr. Hale had already acted suspicious about her connection with Harry, and now he would only have more evidence for his suspicions. He was the only remaining bachelor who she had not yet eliminated—but her hope was scant. Had Harry yet spoken to him as he had planned? Would it matter? If Mr. Hale had just seen her practically rising on her toes to kiss Harry, then he was bound to ignore any of Harry's advice to court her. He would think her a wanton, just like Sir Francis and Mrs. Coleman had assumed.

Emma cleared her throat, the awkwardness in the room too much to bear. "Farewell, gentlemen. I am going to change for dinner." It was the first thing that came to mind. Though dinner was still a few hours away, she didn't care. She curtsied and rushed toward the staircase.

When she made it to her room, she was shocked to find Isabel standing outside of it.

"I'm sorry, miss." Her eyes were round and rueful. "Mrs. Coleman told me to leave ye alone with Sir Francis. 'Twasn't good of me not to tell ye."

Emma frowned. Why would Mrs. Coleman have wanted Emma to be left unchaperoned? Had she hoped Sir Francis would propose? Or had she wanted a reason to have Emma sent away for improper behavior?

A chill ran over her spine. That seemed more like it.

CHAPTER FIFTEEN

"Did I see Sir Francis walking up the staircase with a broken nose?" Mr. Hale asked. His dark green eyes flooded with curiosity as he finally ended the silence in the entry hall. Harry was glad that Sir Francis's nose had claimed more of Mr. Hale's attention than the sight of Harry and Emma standing so close to one another. Still, it could not have escaped his notice.

Mr. Hale was still waiting for a reply, so Harry gave a stiff nod. "You are not mistaken."

"May I ask what caused the injury?"

"His own stupidity." Harry let out a hard laugh. It relieved some of the tension in his shoulders.

Mr. Hale did not seem satisfied with that answer, his curiosity still obvious. He would have to remain curious. Harry could never tell him what had occurred between Emma and Sir Francis, no matter how badly he wished to expose the man's character to everyone who would listen. It would damage Emma's reputation and any remaining chance she had at securing a husband from among the guests.

"Sir Francis has done something unpardonable, and so I have thrown him out." Harry rolled the edges of his sleeves. "That is all."

Mr. Hale seemed to understand not to pry. He gave a slow nod, but his eyes never left Harry's face. "I trust your judgment. The outcome was deserved, I am sure of it." He paused. "Is Miss Eastwood well? She seemed distressed."

Harry searched for an explanation that would leave Mr. Hale free of any suspicion toward her. "Unfortunately Miss Eastwood was unlucky enough to witness my confrontation with Sir Francis. She was upset by the conflict as you might imagine."

Mr. Hale gave him a look of understanding. "Ah. That does make sense."

"I'm sorry you had to witness the aftermath as well."

A slow smile climbed Mr. Hale's face. "I'm always glad to witness a little entertainment. It may be folly to admit it, but I will not be sorry to see Sir Francis go."

Harry chuckled. "Nor will I, obviously."

He remembered his promise to Emma in the library. He needed to encourage Mr. Hale to pursue her. The words tangled in his mouth as he tried to form them. "I daresay Miss Eastwood will be glad to see Sir Francis leave as well. She is a very amiable, proper young woman, and his excessive attention was unsettling to her."

"Was it?" Mr. Hale raised a brow. "She seemed to be enjoying the attention."

"Not from what she has told me. In fact..." Harry paused, debating with himself over how to continue, "...she has confided in me a specific interest in you, Mr. Hale. She finds you very agreeable and much less overbearing."

Mr. Hale interlocked his hands behind his back and looked down at the floor. "Is it your assumption that every man in this house wishes to court Miss Eastwood?"

Harry scowled. How could he answer that question? "Well, the behavior of the men here has led me to believe as much. Ever since she first sang, she has been the center of attention. I do hope she marries, and marries well. She deserves only the best sort of man, and I had reason to hope she might find him among my guests."

Mr. Hale studied Harry for a long moment, his expression unreadable. "Miss Eastwood seems a very sweet young lady, indeed, and I confess myself just as astonished by her talent and beauty as the other men. But your hopes for her marriage...I find them surprising."

"Why?"

Mr. Hale hesitated. "From what few interactions I've witnessed between you and Miss Eastwood, I thought I sensed an attachment between the two of you."

"No, of course not." Harry's instant denial only seemed to make Mr. Hale even more suspicious. By way of defending himself, he almost told Mr. Hale about his engagement, but he stopped himself. "There is no attachment between Miss Eastwood and myself. She has been my friend for many years, and that is the cause of any closeness you may have perceived between us. I view her, wholeheartedly, as I would a sister." He cleared his throat. What a lie. If it would convince Mr. Hale to take a chance to get to know Emma better, then it was worth it.

"Does Miss Eastwood share that view?" Mr. Hale asked in a skeptical voice.

"Yes." A hint of doubt hung in his voice. Harry had always believed Emma's feelings to be indifferent—but he had never asked. He had never opened his heart enough to find out. But now that it was too late, he was finally noticing signs of affection in her voice and eyes and the way she behaved when she was with him—signs that stoked his regret into flames.

"I assure you," Harry continued in as strong a voice as he could muster, "if you made an effort to come to know Miss Eastwood, you would be overwhelmed with all the good you find her to be in possession of." Harry gave a smile that felt like betrayal. "I would encourage you to do so."

Mr. Hale was silent for a long moment, his head tipped slightly in one direction. Did he still not believe Harry? What more could he say?

"I would hate to give Miss Eastwood false expectations," he said finally, his face stoic. "I am not minded to marry at any point in the near future, though I will take your consideration for your friend Miss Eastwood as the highest of compliments."

Harry stared at him in stunned silence for a moment before giving a nod. "That is understandable." But not convenient. He didn't want to see Emma forced to choose between the men she had already found fault with. "What prevents your desire to marry?"

Mr. Hale crossed his arms. "A great number of things." He sighed. "I was once engaged, and circumstances prevented the marriage from taking place. Many would say I should be recovered from the effects by now, but a heart such as mine isn't so easily mended." He gave a lighthearted smile. "The ailment gives me reason to fear the idea of another engagement."

"I cannot blame you." Harry wished there were some circumstances that might prevent him from marrying Miss Fitzroy. He could see no escape. He was bound in honor, and she was so eager to be mistress of Garsley, there was no possible way she would change her mind. His heart ached as he forced his thoughts back to Mr. Hale. "Could nothing ever persuade you to change your opinion on marriage?"

Mr. Hale took a deep breath, his eyes distant. "Only the deepest love, I suppose." Despite the serious nature of the conversation, he gave a cheerful smile. "I'm not certain I would wish such an ailment upon myself again, but I hope love is kinder to you than it has been to me."

Harry tried to smile, but the effort was futile.

Love could not be blamed for putting Emma so far out of reach. He could only blame himself.

Mr. Hale's hair was the color of copper in the candlelight. Emma took a deep breath as she observed him from across the drawing room after dinner. He held a book on his lap, and the other side of the settee where he sat was empty. What did he make of what he had seen earlier that day? The entire household had been buzzing with the news of Sir Francis's abrupt departure, and the overall mood had actually been made more pleasant for it.

Well, aside from Mrs. Coleman's.

Having Sir Francis thrown out of Garsley hadn't been

her plan at all. She had obviously wanted the consequences to fall on Emma. Even now, Mrs. Coleman stared at Emma from her place on the sofa, a complete lack of fondness in her cold expression.

To distract herself, Emma opened the poetry book on her lap. She only read one line before Mr. Seaton interrupted her. "Will you sing for us again, Miss Eastwood?" With Sir Francis out of the way, the attentions of Mr. Seaton had doubled. His dark eyes gleamed with eagerness.

She gave a polite smile. "If you wish."

After his spectacle during the fencing tournament, she hardly dared to refuse his request. He might throw another one of his tantrums. The idea brought a relieving amount of humor to her otherwise anxious demeanor. It had been a terrible, rotten day, and she wished to forget it.

Well, perhaps not all of it.

Her thoughts wandered back to how Harry had held her, his fingers tracing over her lips. She could still feel the weight of his gaze on her, the depth of emotion in it, and the conclusion she had drawn from the entire ordeal had haunted her all evening.

Friends did not look at their friends in such a manner.

She no longer had any doubt that Harry felt something more than friendship for her. The way he had defended her from Sir Francis was still making her heart skip deep inside her chest. She quickly shushed her thoughts. Even though Harry did seem to have feelings for her, they obviously weren't enough. He had still chosen Miss Fitzroy and his hotel, and that hurt Emma perhaps more than if he had never loved her at all.

She couldn't blame him though. She had never made

her feelings known, so he had no reason to hope. Or, if he had taken this long to even recognize his feelings, he would have had nothing to stop him from engaging himself to Miss Fitzroy. The fates were against Emma being with Harry. They had been from the beginning, and she knew, deep in her bones, that that would never change. She needed to cling to the possibility of marrying Mr. Hale with just as much ferocity as she had been clinging to Harry all those years. The shift in her mind and heart was essential, especially now that he was the only remaining bachelor at Garsley who didn't give her an unsettling chill across her spine much like the one Mr. Blyth had given her.

Mr. Seaton called the attention of the room to Emma as she stood to honor his request. She stood near the pianoforte and began singing without any instrument to accompany her. The lyrics had intrigued her from the first moment she had heard her mother sing the song. They spoke of a lost love, likening it to the wind and how it blows carelessly in one part of the world before racing away to the next. At least that was how she had interpreted the vague words of the song. As she had grown up, she hadn't found those words relatable at all. Her love for anyone in her life— her late mother, her father, Harry—didn't blow away as the song suggested. Her love was constant and forever, no matter how much she wished—in Harry's case—that it would pass like a breeze.

By the time she finished singing, her eyes prickled with tears. She swallowed the lump in her throat as she met Harry's gaze from where he stood near the hearth.

His features were solemn, brows drawn together. But

then he smiled as he applauded, and her heart broke a little more.

She let out a shaky breath, gathering her composure. She knew what she needed to do, yet she dreaded it completely. With confident steps, she made her way to the settee where Mr. Hale sat with his book. He observed her approach with an expressionless face, though she sensed his surprise when she sat down beside him.

"Miss Eastwood." He gave a nod in greeting. "That was a remarkable performance, as always."

"Thank you very much, sir." Emma forced her mouth into a smile.

Mr. Hale closed his book, addressing her with a look of concern. "I am glad to see you are improved after the… distressing events of the afternoon."

She felt her skin blanch. Had Harry told him what had happened with Sir Francis? Her reputation would be at stake if word of it reached any other ear in the household. "Distressing events?" she asked with a scowl.

"I was told that you witnessed the discord between Sir Francis and Mr. Coleman. I'm surprised the gentlemen didn't conduct their business without a lady present."

Was that all Harry had told him? That the two men had fought because of their own disagreements? Relief slunk through her. "Ah, yes. I wish I hadn't seen it, but I assure you, I am much recovered now."

"I am glad to hear it." He gave a small smile before falling into silence for several seconds.

Emma searched for something she might ask him to keep their conversation going. "What did you make of the lyrics of the song I sang just now? Everyone seems to have a different opinion of them and their accuracy when it comes to love."

His eyes narrowed in thought. "I found the lyrics to be an an accurate representation of my own experience." There was an edge of bitterness in his voice that surprised her.

"And what experience is this?"

He laughed under his breath. "It is a history that I don't care to relay. Suffice it to say that I have been injured by love in the past, so I will gladly enjoy music that condemns it." His smile softened as he avoided Emma's gaze by looking down at the leather cover of his book.

A bloom of compassion opened in her heart as she stared at his profile. "I too know how it feels to be hurt by love." The pain in her chest had been expanding all day, fortified by the flashes of Harry's solemn eyes and soft smile in the back of her mind.

Mr. Hale glanced up. "Do you?"

"Yes, but 'it is a history that I don't care to relay.'" She threw him a small grin, though she didn't feel it. Unfortunately, the pain love had inflicted on her wasn't yet a part of her history. It was ongoing.

Against her better judgment, her eyes slid in Harry's direction. He was watching her conversation with Mr. Hale. Thankfully, he was too far away to overhear it. Had he spoken to Mr. Hale and encouraged him to court her yet? He did seem a little more keen for conversation that evening. Perhaps it was because Sir Francis was gone. Everyone was much less ill at ease in his absence.

When she glanced at Mr. Hale again, her stomach sank. He had followed her gaze to Harry, who was now watching her with no small measure of suspicion. She chose to ignore it, angling her body more toward him to show that he had her full attention. "I suppose we have something in common after all, Mr. Hale."

"It seems we do." His smile seemed forced as he returned his attention to his book again. It was obvious that he didn't wish to continue the conversation. She shrunk with defeat and clasped her hands together in her lap. It made sense that not all five bachelors would be interested in her. She had been surprised to find *any* of them so smitten, so she shouldn't have been disappointed that Mr. Hale had no particular attention to give her. Were her efforts entirely futile? Or was she just doing something wrong?

When the guests began to retire for the evening, Emma was one of the first to stand. Her head ached from her crying earlier that day, and all she wanted to do was sink into her pillows and drift off to sleep where she could forget her failures. She breezed past Harry as quickly as she could, desperate to avoid any further interaction with him. She felt his gaze on her back as she went through the door and hurried through the corridors to the staircase.

Once she was safely inside her room, she called for Isabel to come help her undress. Isabel was more quiet than usual as she braided Emma's hair and took her leave. With her hair braided, her night clothes on, and her eyelids drooping, Emma staggered toward her bed to climb under the blanket.

Just before she blew out the candle at her bedside, a knock on her door made her jump. She tugged the blanket up under her chin, heart pounding. It wasn't Isabel's knock.

"Who is it?" Emma asked after a few seconds.

A deep female voice met her ears. "Mrs. Coleman."

Emma shifted in her bed, sitting up straighter. What on earth was Harry's mother doing at her room so late at night? "Y-you may enter."

Instantly, the door opened and Mrs. Coleman swept inside. She stopped a few paces away from Emma's bed, one eyebrow arched menacingly. "Did you think you could so easily escape my reprimand?"

"Pardon me?" Emma held tightly to the edge of the blanket.

Mrs. Coleman's chest heaved with a quaking breath. "Your behavior today with Sir Francis was entirely unacceptable. Isabel has informed me of the entire ordeal, of how you sent her away so you could be alone with him. Not only is such impropriety unacceptable at Garsley, but then your actions provoked Harry enough to send his most eager investor away with a broken nose." She touched her forehead as she composed herself. "I hope you are sorry." Her eyes flashed in the dim candlelight.

Isabel's story had been quite different. Emma didn't want the girl to be punished for telling Emma the truth, so she couldn't accuse Mrs. Coleman, no matter how much she wanted to. Emma took a deep breath, a new surge of anxiousness overtaking her. "Sir Francis was the only one who behaved dishonorably. I'm sorry Harry lost the investor. It was Harry's decision to send him away, though I am sorry to have been involved." She swallowed. "At least you may still depend upon Miss Fitzroy to bring the bulk of the funds."

Mrs. Coleman took a step closer, and the angry gleam in her eyes reminded Emma of Arabella. "May I? May I depend upon such a thing, or will you ruin that as well?"

Emma exhaled sharply. "You may depend upon the marriage between your son and Miss Fitzroy, ma'am. I have no intention of coming between them, as I have said many times." She tried to keep her voice calm, but that was becoming increasingly difficult.

Mrs. Coleman's neck was red with anger, though her expression remained eerily calm. "I hope you are true to your word, Miss Eastwood. Or I shall think even less of you than I already do."

Her words hung in the air as she turned on her heel and took her leave.

Emma stared at the door as it clicked shut behind her. The tension in her shoulders lowered, but her heart stung. No matter where Emma went, there was always someone to make it abundantly clear that she was unwelcome. That she didn't belong.

That she was a burden.

After her conversation with Mr. Hale that night, her hope for finding a husband among the guests had practically withered to nothing. What use was there for her to stay at Garsley any longer? Her singing was all she had, and a future in London as a performer seemed imminent. Staying at Garsley at this point was only prolonging the inevitable. She was losing investors for Harry, she was distressing Mrs. Coleman greatly, and seeing Harry every day, knowing he could never be hers, was causing more harm than good. Her presence there might have even been distracting him from his upcoming marriage. She couldn't do that.

She couldn't make Mrs. Coleman's claims correct.

Her lungs felt heavy as she blew out her candle and

settled into her pillows. She was no longer tired. She was wide awake for hours until she came to her final decision.

She had to leave Garsley. She would speak with Harry the next day. If he could provide her passage to London, she would fend for herself from that moment onward.

A pang of grief was the last thing she felt before she drifted to sleep.

CHAPTER SIXTEEN

Sea birds flew amid the distant trees, crossing the morning sky in streaks of white. Emma wrapped her cloak more tightly around herself, keeping out the cold breeze as best she could. Harry hadn't been at breakfast, so she had looked for him in his study. He hadn't been there either, nor the library. She couldn't very well ask Mrs. Coleman if she knew where he had gone, so she thought to go searching for him instead. Her resolve to leave Garsley had remained strong all morning. It was the only decision she could feel at peace with. She had never planned to come to Garsley at all. To return to her original plan of singing in London should have been easy, but instead she felt terrified.

Even so, staying was no longer an option. There was nothing for her at Garsley. Nothing but heartbreak and disappointment.

Could London really be any worse?

She stopped in front of the keep, brushing a strand of her wind-blown hair out of her face. Harry must have been inside. It seemed to be a morning routine of his, to go there to make his plans and dreams.

She looked up at the impressive stone structure. It towered up and up, with more birds circling around the top. She could easily envision guests from all over England coming to stay in such an incredible historic structure. It was ancient and mysterious on the outside, but would be beautiful and comfortably furnished on the inside with a view of the coast that was even more breathtaking. She could see why Harry was so in love with the idea. It would bring him a great deal of income and connections. It was brilliant, and the sort of thing that would make him truly happy for years to come.

She felt ill as she opened the door with its broken lock. She started up the steep stone staircase, following the spiral until she reached the first level. "Harry?" she called out.

From the floor above, she heard his confused voice. "Emma?"

Her heart leaped. She had known he would be there. "I-I'm coming up." A jolt of nerves tugged at her stomach, but she hurried toward the next set of stairs. These ones felt steeper than the last set. When she reached the corridor on the second floor, she caught sight of Harry through the open doorway. The floor covered in his design plans, the papers strewn all around the first room. He stood with a piece of chalk in his hand, his hair mussed.

He smiled, his eyes slightly dazed as they settled on her face. "Emma. What brings you out here?"

"I wished to speak with you," she said in a timid voice.

"It is a steep climb, is it not?" He dropped the chalk to the floor and dusted off his hands as he strode toward her.

"Indeed." She was still catching her breath. "It would seem my legs are not as strong as I thought they were."

Harry's eyes danced with amusement. "Don't forget you walked eighteen miles to get here."

She gave a modest smile. "It was no easy task, I assure you. I was sore for days."

Harry chuckled, pushing the hair off his brow and straightening his jacket. "I suspect I'll be sore from stooping down to do all this mapping." He gestured toward the numerous chalk marks that covered the stone floor. "I've been marking where all the furniture will be placed and the walls erected so I can envision it better."

Emma's heart sank a little. She had wondered if perhaps he was beginning to regret his choice to marry Miss Fitzroy, but it seemed he was still fixated on his hotel plans. Mrs. Coleman was wrong to be so worried.

"These rooms will attract many guests, I am sure of it," Emma said in an encouraging voice.

Harry's brow twinged as he stared down at the floor. "That is the hope."

Emma twisted her fingers together. How should she begin? Her mind raced. "There is a matter I wished to speak with you about."

Harry's worried expression turned to her face. "Go on."

She took a deep breath. "After the events of yesterday, and witnessing yet again Mr. Hale's disinterest in courting me, I—well I have come to the decision that I would like to leave Garsley and go to London as I originally planned." Her eyes flickered away from his. "I have come to ask if you would be willing to lend me the funds necessary to travel there and live for a few weeks before I secure work. I would repay you, of course, the very moment I obtain the money." When she looked at his face again, his mouth was a firm line, his brows tilting downward.

"Emma—" He paused, a shaky exhale escaping his lungs. "That cannot be what you truly want. I won't see you off to London alone. It isn't proper." He shook his head. "It isn't safe."

"Singing is all I can do," she said in a choked whisper. "I cannot rely on the goodwill of others to survive any longer. You have a wedding approaching. If we are honest with ourselves, *I* most certainly do not have a wedding in my future. I have exhausted my efforts on Mr. Hale for long enough, and I would rather be a prima donna than the wife of one of the other men here who I hold no regard for."

Harry took a step closer to where she stood in the middle of the stone floor. "That doesn't matter." He raised his eyebrows as he tipped his head down to look at her. "You can stay here until the next Season. I will fund it myself."

Emma exhaled in frustration. "No, I *can't*. I'm not yours to defend and look after. Your responsibility is only for your mother and soon Miss Fitzroy."

Harry looked like he had been struck, his eyes flooding with sorrow.

"I cannot be here when you are married." She shook her head fast. "I know what that is like. I know how it feels to creep through the corridors of a house when the other inhabitants want nothing more than to see me gone." A lump formed in her throat, but she refused to cry in front of Harry again.

His brow contracted, a desperation entering his voice. "The circumstances wouldn't be the same as they were when you lived with your stepbrother. I would ensure you were treated with respect. If it would make you more comfortable, you could stay in one of the rooms in the gatehouse."

Emma gave him a firm look, her frustration growing along with the lump in her throat. "I cannot."

"Why?"

She threw her hands in the air in front of her. "Because it would hurt far too much to see you every day!" Her face burned the moment the confession escaped her, but the words had come fast and without permission. He stared at her, but she could hardly meet his gaze. Though she was embarrassed by her confession, it was also empowering. She took a deep, shaky breath, her voice barely a whisper. "To live alone in a London apartment, singing for strangers, facing the scrutiny of the papers, living on meager wages— all of that would be far easier than seeing you married to Miss Fitzroy." What was she doing? She was admitting her feelings without *actually* admitting them. What she was insinuating was not what she had intended when she had come to the keep. All she had meant to do was tell him that she was leaving.

She watched his boots step closer. "Do you think it's been easy for me?" His gruff voice brought a flutter to her stomach.

Her gaze jerked up to his, her heart thudding. "What?"

"Do you think it's been easy to watch five men descend upon Garsley and compete for your attention? To-to *encourage* them to do so? To watch you flirt with them? To imagine that one of them might marry you?"

She shook her head in confusion. "Was it not your idea?

You have been encouraging me to pursue Mr. Hale from the start. And why should it vex you to see me flirting with other men?" she scoffed. "*You* are the one who is engaged." Her face heated with anger and raw emotion. "If the thought of me marrying another man vexes you so greatly, then why did you never ask me yourself?"

Silence fell between them, and a hot tear trickled down her cheek. She swiped it away as she caught her breath. A sob clenched her stomach, but she held it back. What had possessed her? Why was she speaking so freely?

Harry's chest rose and fell with a heavy breath. "I didn't know you felt this way."

Emma blinked fast, staring at the floor. When she spoke, it was barely a whisper. "How could you not know?" Her heartbeat echoed in her ears, fast and shallow. "When my valise was stolen, along with everything I own, the items I mourned the most were your letters. I kept every one. I treasured them." She wiped at her cheek. "When my mother died and I moved away from the only home I had ever known, you were all I had to look forward to." Emma couldn't stop the sob that shook her frame. "You were all I had to love." Her heart was on fire. It was useless to try to stop it.

Finally, Harry spoke again, and his voice touched every inch of her skin. "I never asked how you felt." He gave a gruff sigh. "I never told you how I felt either."

Emma dared to look up at him. The shock that coursed through her was nothing to the longing that swirled around her heart, dipping and soaring through her stomach until she could scarcely draw a breath.

She saw the same thing reflected in his eyes.

He touched her face, his fingertips running circles across her cheek and the side of her hair. He leaned his forehead against hers, his hands encircling her waist. "I should have told you a long time ago," he whispered. "I—"

"Do not say it, Harry." Emma swallowed hard against the lump in her throat. "You are not at liberty to make any declarations to me. You are too late."

He leaned back enough to look into her eyes. His features were sodden with frustration, his brows drawn together in regret. He looked so sad—so broken. "Stay," he said in a hoarse voice. "Please."

"To what end? You know why I must leave. You know as well as I that I cannot live within these walls."

"You can if you're my wife."

Her eyes rounded, her heart racing. "Harry—"

"I'll inform Miss Fitzroy of my decision to break off the engagement. Word should easily reach her before she begins her journey to Garsley. If I can spare her the long journey, she might come to forgive me."

Emma stared up at him, a mixture of guilt and terror and overwhelming joy battling inside her. What had she done? Mrs. Coleman would have her head. Emma's frantic thoughts refused to cease. "I thought you were determined to keep your word."

He brushed her hair aside with a gentle touch that sent a shiver across her neck. "In this instance, I can either be a man of my word, or of my heart. I cannot be both. My heart is yours, Emma." His voice broke. "It always has been. I must finally be true to it."

Her eyelids were heavy, her heart beating so quickly it brought a lightness to her head. It surprised her then, that she still had enough strength to rise on her toes and begin kissing him as if she were far more practiced that Sir Francis had described her to be.

Though she had started it, Harry didn't hesitate. He pulled her against him, his fingertips pressing into her back. She felt the movement of his jaw under her palms, the unexpected stubble on his face rough and abrasive against her lips. She didn't care. Her entire body was melting into a puddle, waves of desire crashing through her like the waves against the rocks that could be seen from the window. Her heart soared like the birds that circled the keep. Harry's lashes, closed against his cheek, were like their wings.

Her eyes fell closed, the sensations of Harry's kisses making her lightheaded. Still, she was an active participant, powerless to walk away. She held tight to his lapels, pulling him impossibly closer. Though her mind pestered her with alarms, her heart would not be told. She loved him. This was what Harry had meant when he said that when she kissed the right man, she would not hate it. The contrast between this moment and Sir Francis's kiss was almost impossible to believe.

His hands left her waist, burying into her hair and encircling her cheeks as he kissed her with renewed fervor, deepening their kiss and throwing open the gates that held the last of her emotions. This couldn't go on, no matter how beautiful and wonderful it was.

It took all of her effort, but she tore her mouth away from his. "Harry—" Emma took a gasp for the air she had been lacking moments before. She shook her head fast. "I did not come here to try to change your mind. I came to tell you that I wished to leave." Her voice faded as his deep brown eyes sank into hers.

"Marry me, Emma." The sincerity in his gaze unraveled her resolve.

"You cannot say such things until your business with Miss Fitzroy is settled." With great effort, she took one large step away from him. Her lips tingled and burned from his kiss. Had it been real? His chestnut hair was tousled, and she could still see the creases in his lapels that had been balled up in her fists. It *had* been real, yet forbidden and cruel all the same.

Fear overwhelmed her senses.

How could she trust that he wouldn't change his mind again? He had known Emma his entire life. If he could choose Miss Fitzroy once in a weak moment of ambition, then surely he could choose her again. Once he came back to his senses and realized that Emma could give him none of the dreams he desired, he would abandon her. He would realize his mistake.

Emma took another step away, crossing her arms to keep her emotions together.

Harry's gaze was determined, but he respected the space she had created. He remained where he stood. "I will ensure it is settled at once."

"Think on it a little longer, please." Emma cast him a desperate look. How could she rob him of his dreams? How could she be so selfish? "Do not act rashly."

"I'm not." Harry started to walk toward her again, but she panicked, her heart racing with regret.

"We should not be here alone," she blurted. If he came close enough, she would undoubtedly want to kiss him again. "I should go." She backed away and then whirled around as fast as she could. The steep stairs were no match for her eagerness to escape Harry and the wild emotions he had awoken inside her. She was impressed by her own agility as she descended the steps and strode out onto the lawn as quickly as her legs could carry her.

Catching her breath was difficult in the fierce wind that whipped at her face and dress. She squinted in the sunlight, her vision flooding with tears. What had just passed between her and Harry could either be the happiest or most painful moment of her life. She couldn't yet decide which it was, but she knew in her bones that she would feel the impact of it forever.

She hadn't even intended to come to Garsley in the first place, and now she was causing all sorts of upheaval. She thought she had lost everything—including Harry—but now there was a bud of hope inside her, struggling to bloom amid all her uncertainty. If she ever dared to hope for any good thing, she always seemed to lose it. Why should this be any different? Why should she believe Harry meant what he said? When he had a chance to think logically, how could he not renounce those words and that kiss they had just shared in favor of the hotel plans he had invested so much in?

She had just promised Mrs. Coleman the night before that she wouldn't come between Harry and Miss Fitzroy. Harry's words echoed in her mind. *In this instance, I can either be a man of my word, or of my heart. I cannot be both.* Was the same true for her? After Mrs. Coleman's attempts to ruin Emma's reputation with Sir Francis, Emma should not have been concerned about pleasing Mrs. Coleman. Why should she not claim her own chance at happiness?

She circled the castle twice before her emotions were somewhat composed. With a deep breath, she walked inside, brushing her wind blown hair out of her face. To her dismay, Mrs. Coleman stood inside the entry hall, along with two other women Emma didn't recognize. Mrs. Coleman didn't often receive friends, so Emma was surprised to see them standing there, white muslin skirts brushing the checkered floors.

More surprising than the visitors though, was Mrs. Coleman's gleeful expression as she turned toward the sound of Emma's footsteps.

Emma gave a tight smile. Did she look like she had just been crying? Or worse—that she had just been thoroughly kissed?

"Miss Eastwood, come meet the newest guests of Garsley." The friendly tone in Mrs. Coleman's voice was almost more frightening than when she had censored Emma in her room the night before.

Emma tried to hide the confusion from her brow as she walked forward. At the closer view, Emma noted that one woman appeared to be close to Mrs. Coleman's age, while the other was much younger. Her dark hair was almost black, pulled tight into a knot at the crown of her head. Her eyes were also dark, framed in curled lashes and striking brows.

Mrs. Coleman waited until Emma was directly beside her, and there was a gleam of triumph in her eyes. "Miss Eastwood, allow me to introduce Lady Burgess and her daughter, Miss Daphne Fitzroy."

CHAPTER SEVENTEEN

Harry paced all over the chalk lines he had drawn in the keep, smudging the hours of work he had just completed. It no longer mattered. All his plans for the hotel, all the days he had wasted dreaming of something that wouldn't make him truly happy, had lost all their importance.

Emma loved him. He was sure of it now.

And he loved her more than he had ever loved anything or anyone.

That was *all* that mattered.

His heart raced as he considered the best possible way to move forward. Emma still doubted him—she had run away. He couldn't blame her for being cautious. He didn't expect to win her trust all at once. He needed to prove to her that he was going to follow through on his promise to end his engagement and the entire business arrangement with Miss Fitzroy. The thought was already relieving a weight on his shoulders. His body thrummed with nervousness, but that was nothing beside the emotional chaos that Emma's kiss had caused inside him. When they were young, he had hoped to be her first kiss. Sir Francis had stolen that honor, but Harry could only hope that he would be her last. He was still reeling from the sensation of holding her in his arms and kissing her—and from seeing the spark of hope in her eyes when he told her he would break off his engagement.

He caught his breath, reining in his emotions for long enough to focus on the task at hand. The first item of business would be to write a letter to Miss Fitzroy. After that, he would reveal the news to his mother. He was dreading that conversation most of all. And then, with any luck, his devotion would be proven to Emma and she might forgive him for being an insufferable fool. He would then send all the bachelors back to their homes and far away from Emma.

The relief he felt at that prospect was overwhelming.

Lastly, he would properly ask Emma to marry him as he should have done a long time ago.

His determination surged as he looked at his smudged drawings on the floor of the keep. Knowing that Emma was on the other side of his decision made leaving his dream of the hotel behind much less difficult. Still, he took a moment to bury the idea in the past. It was acceptable to mourn it. The grief he felt was nothing to the sense of peace that followed his new decision. Emma was worth any sacrifice.

He hurried down the stairs and out into the cold spring breeze. He strode into the entry hall, stopping abruptly in his tracks at the scene in front of him.

"Ah, there you are." Mother strode forward, arms outstretched. She took his arm and pulled him forward.

Harry blinked, scowling until the other three women came into focus.

Miss Fitzroy was there.

Her dark, striking features were unmistakable, and her mother, Lady Burgess's face also rang with familiarity. Her dark hair was streaked in grey, much like his own mother's, but Lady Burgess stood much taller like her daughter. What on earth was Miss Fitzroy doing here already? She had told him she would be arriving several weeks from that date. Dread fell through his stomach.

Emma stood nearby, her posture so stiff that her shoulder blades pinched together. She took a deep breath, her gaze flickering to Harry for a short moment before returning to the floor again. Her blonde hair had fallen halfway out of its arrangement, which could have been due to the wind, but Harry likely owned more of the blame. She must have been mortified to be presenting herself to Lady Burgess and Miss Fitzroy in such a state.

He let out a tense breath, offering a bow. "Lady Burgess, Miss Fitzroy. I confess myself surprised to see you here so soon."

Lady Burgess laughed, a high-pitched trill. "Did your mother not tell you?"

Harry raised his brows, forcing a polite smile to remain on his face. "Tell me what?"

Lady Burgess exchanged a glance with Mother, who took a quick step forward. "Oh, yes, forgive me." She chuckled. "It completely slipped my mind. I neglected to inform you that I wrote to Lady Burgess about three weeks ago and invited her and Miss Fitzroy to come sooner. I hoped to acquaint myself with them before we were in the throes of wedding planning."

Harry stared at her in shock. Three weeks? That must have been around the time Emma arrived at Garsley. If his mother had seen Emma as a threat to his engagement to Miss Fitzroy, then it made sense that she would have plotted to have her arrive sooner. His chest tightened with frustration.

Mother gave a broad smile, as if she *hadn't* just revealed some wicked scheme. She turned toward Lady Burgess and Miss Fitzroy again. "I must have forgotten to inform him because I was distracted by our many guests. Besides Miss Eastwood, we also have five—er—*four* young gentlemen at Garsley who are interested in investing in the hotel."

"Oh, dear," Lady Burgess frowned. "I hope we haven't come at an inconvenient time, Mr. Coleman. Although, we have no intention of leaving at this point," she added with a laugh. "That was a long, arduous five days in a carriage." She sighed. "I should never like to sleep at a coaching inn again. They are not nearly as comfortable as your hotel at Garsley is sure to be." She and mother gave gleeful laughs in unison, and Miss Fitzroy beamed with pride.

Harry could have sank into the floor. He studied Emma's profile. Her cheeks were flushed. She gave an abrupt curtsy. "Please excuse me," she muttered.

Harry flinched toward her, almost grabbing her arm to stop her. He wanted to reassure her that he would find a way out of this, but she was already through the doorway and outside again. The other three women hardly blinked at her departure, continuing on with their conversation.

"...nevertheless, the journey was well worth it," Lady

Burgess said. "I would travel any distance if it is for the purpose of my only daughter's wedding. We planned many of the details during our travels."

"Did you now?" Mother asked with a grin. "I look forward to hearing what you have planned."

Lady Burgess leaned forward, covering half her mouth with her fingertips. "Well, we have already had the dress made and have brought it with us. You have never seen such a pretty thing in your life. I shall not shock you with the price, but my dear Daphne looks so lovely in it that I find the money well spent indeed." She turned toward Harry. "I suspect you are most eager to see her in the gown, aren't you, Mr. Coleman?"

Harry swallowed, giving a stiff nod. "Of course." What else could he say? He couldn't very well break off the engagement with Miss Fitzroy right there in front of their mothers. He needed to find a private moment to speak to her. He was drowning in anxiousness as the women continued to speak of the wedding plans—which had been made in great detail.

Miss Fitzroy watched him as their mothers continued their prattle. Her dark eyes, nearly black, were inquisitive. She had always been polite, quiet, and more inclined to listen than to speak. Their mothers were much louder, dominating the conversation. Harry was desperate to go reassure Emma. He could imagine her hiding in her room, believing him to be a cad who had used her as Sir Francis had. His heart pinched with dread.

With a quick bow, he attempted to sneak away toward the door, but Mother stopped him, pausing her conversation with Lady Burgess. "Harry! Where are you going? You would be a cruel host not to offer Lady Burgess and your betrothed a tour of her future home."

Harry closed his eyes, drawing a deep breath before turning around. He hadn't the slightest idea of the most delicate way to break off an engagement, especially on the very day of their arrival. He would be the very definition of a cruel host if he did that.

He needed to think. If there was a way to express his change of plans to Miss Fitzroy that would cause her minimal embarrassment, then he needed to wait for that moment. A tour of the castle with her mother and his mother in tow was *not* that moment.

He nodded as graciously as he could, but all he could think of was Emma and what she must have been thinking. He would find time to speak with her that day. He had to.

"Wonderful," Lady Burgess said, her lips pulling into a rapturous smile. "I shall see all that my daughter is to be mistress of."

Harry cringed inwardly, his heart picking up speed as Miss Fitzroy walked forward and took his arm. "I too shall see it for the first time." Her lashes blinked up at him. "I hope it is all you described it to be."

He struggled to form words amid the storm of guilt in his chest. "You might be disappointed."

"I'm certain I won't be." She lifted her chin as Harry began what he hoped would be a short tour.

Emma didn't stop walking until she reached the other side of the hill beyond the moat and bridge. Thankfully, it hadn't rained in days, so there wasn't any mud on the grassy slope. Behind the hill, Garsley was out of sight. She could almost forget that it was there and that Harry was inside with Miss Fitzroy and her mother at that very moment. The fact that Mrs. Coleman had secretly invited them to come sooner didn't surprise Emma one bit.

She let out a huffed breath, burying her face in her hands as the wind whipped through her skirts. She sat down at the base of the hill. She couldn't go back inside. There was a trap set for her there by Mrs. Coleman, as if she were a rat in the kitchens. She felt much safer outside, even if the wind was bitter cold.

She uncovered her face and wrapped her arms around herself, pulling her cloak tighter. What would Harry do? What would he say? If he broke off his engagement now, after Miss Fitzroy had traveled so far, it would be an even harsher impertinence than it would have been if he had written to her before she left. What little hope Harry's declarations that day—and his kiss—had given her, withered into nothing. He couldn't turn back on his promise now. He would see sense, and Emma would no longer have to feel like she had ruined the plans of so many people.

That was all she did, wasn't it? Ruined things? She had ruined Arabella's happiness by being in her house. She had ruined her stepbrother's freedom when he had been forced to take her in. If she encouraged Harry to break off his engagement, she would ruin his dreams and damage Miss Fitzroy's reputation. Mrs. Coleman would never forgive her for it.

As she fretted over all the reasons she could never set foot in Garsley again, she also rebelliously thought of her kiss with Harry over and over again. It wasn't wise to do so, but she couldn't help it. She had never felt anything more perfect.

Amid her thoughts, she caught sight of a man astride a dark brown horse in the distance. As he rode closer, she realized it was Mr. Hale. She quickly stood and brushed the grass from her cloak, tucking her undone hair behind her ear. Even though she no longer had any hope or desire of capturing his attention, she didn't want to look like a wild thing in front of him.

Mr. Hale slowed his horse's gait, coming to a stop just in front of her. The wind had undone the usually neat appearance of his hair, leaving the short auburn strands to toil freely around his face. "Miss Eastwood." He loosened the reins when his horse tossed its head in annoyance. Mr. Hale's brow furrowed. "What are you doing out here in the wind?"

"I could ask the same of you." Emma gave a half smile. It was all she could muster.

"*I'm* returning from town. You were sitting on the grass all alone."

She could hardly hear him over the wind, and she doubted he would hear her reply. "I needed to be alone."

Mr. Hale studied her for a long moment from atop his horse. "Is something amiss?"

Drat. He had heard her after all. "Not at all," she said, crossing her arms more tightly. "I found myself...interrupting the welcome of the Colemans' new guests, so I thought it best to leave them in peace for a time."

"New guests?" Mr. Hale raised his eyebrows. "Are there not enough men here already?"

Emma laughed. "These two guests are women." The wind threw her hair into her face, but she pushed it aside. Harry had yet to tell the men about his engagement, but surely the truth would have to come out now that Miss Fitzroy was here at the same time as the men. How did Mrs. Coleman plan to explain that?

"Women? That is a change, indeed." Mr. Hale looked in the direction of the castle. "Are they friends of Mrs. Coleman's?"

"Y-yes? Yes." Emma cleared her throat. That was a reasonable explanation. "They are Lady Burgess and her daughter Miss Daphne Fitzroy."

Mr. Hale's gaze jerked in Emma's direction with surprise. He shifted on the saddle, a crease appearing between his brows.

"Do you know them?" she asked.

He opened his mouth to speak, then closed it again. He nodded. "We are acquainted, yes."

He had always been quite vague, but he seemed unsettled by the names—almost as unsettled as Emma had been to find Miss Fitzroy in the entry hall. She watched him as he stared at the castle, his eyes distant beneath those furrowed brows. His chest rose and fell quickly, and even his horse seemed to sense his unrest.

"Perhaps you should go offer them a greeting," Emma suggested in a cautious voice. "I presume they would be glad to see you again."

He looked down, his jaw tensing. "I think I will stay outside a little longer."

Emma couldn't help her curiosity. "What reason do you have to avoid them?"

"What reason do you have?" he asked. It was wicked of him to throw the question back at her like that. "Are you not also outside to avoid the new guests?"

"Well..." She searched for an explanation, but he stopped her.

"We shall allow them to get settled in without interruption. Good day, Miss Eastwood." He gave a quick nod of his head in her direction before kicking his heels and sending his horse into motion. What on earth was wrong?

She watched with curiosity as Mr. Hale rode away, sending his horse into a full gallop across the open field. Watching that horse run was tempting her to do the same. If she ran away from castle just as she had run away from Arabella and Tom, she might save herself—and especially Harry—from making a difficult, painful decision. She might save Miss Fitzroy from disappointment.

She closed her eyes as nervousness overwhelmed her heart. Someone was bound to be painfully disappointed either way.

CHAPTER EIGHTEEN

Harry tugged his cravat from his neck in one swift motion, releasing a long exhale as he turned toward the mirror in his bedchamber.

Emma hadn't been at dinner.

Her maid had excused her as not feeling well, but he knew better. He hadn't seen Emma since that morning when he had kissed her and made promises that he was intent on keeping. His heart was raw, his head aching from the worries of the day. Candles flickered on his desk and on the mantle above the hearth, but he couldn't bring himself to blow them out. He couldn't leave Emma to endure a sleepless night, wondering if he had reconsidered what he had said to her that day.

Sneaking into her room would be a great risk, but he knew that he also wouldn't sleep unless he saw her again. He bit his lip, scowling at the floor as he considered how best to proceed. The other guests had already retired for the evening, as well as most of the servants, at least based on the silence from outside his door. Emma's bedchamber was on the floor above his, along with the rooms where the housekeeper had placed Miss Fitzroy and Lady Burgess.

Harry took a candle from his desk and stepped quietly into the corridor. There was no one in sight. He made his way up the staircase and took the sharp right turn toward the corridor where Emma's room was located. Very little light came through the window at the end of the corridor, just a hint of moonlight spilling onto the cushioned window seat. He stopped outside Emma's door. He hadn't thought past that moment. If he was trying to be discreet, he couldn't knock, but he also couldn't open the door without doing so.

Candlelight spilled through the cracks in the door, telling him that she was still awake. Perhaps a quiet knock? His heart raced with sudden nervousness as he struck his knuckles softly against the door three times. "Emma?" he whispered in the dark. He knew she would recognize his voice at least.

He glanced down the corridor to ensure it was still empty. After a few seconds, he heard the latch on the door. It opened a crack and Emma's face appeared. Her eyes were wide with shock. "Harry—what are you doing?"

He held a finger to his lips, glancing over his shoulder before slipping inside. He closed the door behind him. The tension in his muscles relaxed as he turned to face her. "I had to speak with you."

Emma blinked fast, clutching the sides of her cloak. She must have thrown it over her nightdress before answering the door. Her golden hair was in a braid over her right shoulder, her cheeks flushed red. Seeing her in her bedchamber late at night perhaps hadn't been his wisest decision. He had been thinking about their kiss all day. The dim candlelight of the room against Emma's skin and hair and round blue eyes had him distracted from his purpose in coming there.

Her brow contracted into a scowl. "You gave me a great fright by whispering my name outside my door, you know."

"I'm sorry." He smiled. "I was trying to be discreet."

"You are fortunate I recognized your voice, or I might have thrust the poker through the door." She gestured at the sharp metal tool by the hearth.

Despite all the worries of the day, he couldn't help but laugh. "My apologies."

She stared up at him, and he could practically see the defenses she had placed between them. Her features were reserved and cautious.

"I missed you at dinner," he said.

Emma shifted on her feet. "Was I the only one absent?"

"Mr. Hale also kept away from the guests for the evening."

"Did he?" Emma paused. "He was acting strange earlier when he learned that Miss Fitzroy and Lady Burgess had arrived."

Harry frowned. "I wonder why."

"I haven't the slightest idea," Emma muttered. Her eyes were fixed on Harry now. The shock in her gaze had subsided, leaving behind a nervous look. "You didn't have to come here to tell me your decision, Harry. I understand that

Miss Fitzroy's arrival changes the circumstances. She has traveled far. You must follow through with your marriage to her." Her neck was tense as she held her chin up. The threat of tears lingered in her eyes. She still doubted him. His heart stung as she rambled on. "I have accepted it. You ought not to be here. If you are seen leaving my room..."

Harry took two long strides toward her, taking her face between his hands. "Emma." He shook his head. "I no longer have any intention of marrying Miss Fitzroy." He ran his fingers over her flushed cheeks, smoothing away the furrow on her brow with his thumb.

She breathed quickly, closing her eyes. "Not even now that she is here?"

He leaned his forehead against hers. "I meant what I said today. Every word." He kissed each of her eyelids slowly, brushing his nose against hers as he whispered, "I love you. I have been in love with you since before I even knew what that meant." He took her hands. Her small fingers were limp at first, but then they wrapped around his with surprising firmness. He leaned back to look in her eyes.

Her gaze clung to his face, a flicker of hope in it. "But— how do you plan to break off the engagement now that she is here? And her mother is here? Did you hear them today? They have planned the entire wedding." Her brows contracted again. "I cannot be the cause of such upheaval."

He shook his head. "You are not to blame. I am the only one at fault, and I bear all the responsibility of my decision as well as the consequences."

Emma looked down at the floor. "Are you certain you fully understand the consequences?" Her breath shook on the way out. "How could I take your fondest dream from you?" Her hoarse whisper broke his heart. "I would never forgive myself, and I fear..." she took a deep breath, "I fear y-you would one day come to regret your choice."

He softly nudged her chin up with his knuckle, leaning his head down to look in her eyes. "*You* are my fondest dream. Nothing could make me happier than to have you living within these walls, laughing with me, beating me in cards, and destroying my pride each time I wear my spectacles."

She gaze up at him, her liquid eyes nearly spilling over. "I would happily do so," she said around a breathless laugh.

Harry smiled, the anxiety of the day fading as he stared at her face. "As soon as I find a proper moment alone with Miss Fitzroy, I will tell her that I cannot follow through with the wedding."

"That will not be an easy conversation."

"But it will be worth it."

The skin on Emma's cheek was soft beneath his hand as he traced the curve of it. Her dazed eyes drifted to his lips. His heart thudded as he leaned closer, sliding his fingertips into the hair behind her neck. He felt the breath behind her words brushing against his lips. "Don't forget you are still engaged." The tip of her nose feathered against his before she pushed her palms against his chest. He staggered back a step, relieved to find her smiling. Her cheeks were perhaps more flushed than before. "You should go."

She was right. It wasn't fair to Miss Fitzroy for him to be sneaking around, stealing kisses from Emma when Miss Fitzroy still believed he was going to marry her. She didn't deserve to be so mistreated. He had never detected that she had any feelings for Harry, but what if she did? How would she feel if she knew that he had kissed Emma that morning? He needed to put it all to rights. The engagement had been a secret from all the bachelors at Garsley, and he had spoken to his mother that evening about how he intended to keep it that way. He hadn't told her that he planned to break it off —he didn't want to inspire her anger prematurely—but he hoped that he could end the arrangement before it was publicized to their guests.

"Will you come to breakfast tomorrow?" Harry asked as he moved toward the door.

Emma's shy eyes met his as she bit her lower lip. Devil take it, how could she remind him not to kiss her and then proceed to look at him like that? "I will consider it," she said finally. "I just—I fear your mother is trying to drive me away."

Harry shook his head. His mother had never been kind to Emma. "All the more reason for you to be at breakfast."

Emma sighed, wringing her hands together. "We must not give anyone the impression that...that we..." her voice trailed off.

"That we are in love?" Harry couldn't stop his smile.

"Yes," Emma breathed amid a laugh, her cheeks flushing again. "We cannot give anyone reason to be suspicious. We mustn't even look at one another if I come to breakfast."

Harry couldn't stop looking at her now, bathed in candlelight and smiling up at him. "That will be difficult."

She covered her face with her hands, turning her back to him. He laughed at her embarrassment. It was far too endearing.

She walked toward her bed, throwing him a smile over

her shoulder that set his heart pounding again. "Goodnight, Harry."

He didn't want to leave, but he needed to. Nothing good would come from staying a moment longer. "Goodnight, Emma." He backed toward the door, finally tearing his gaze away from her and slipping into the dark corridor.

CHAPTER NINETEEN

I
t was a shame that Miss Fitzroy was so agreeable. Emma sat beside her at the dining table at breakfast, the guilt in her stomach making it difficult to eat more than a few bites. Miss Fitzroy had obviously been brought up with far greater education than Emma had. From the way she spoke to the way she held her head and her fork, she was perfectly refined. She was polite and kind toward Emma, offering her sympathies about Emma's lack of a family and somehow managing to not sound pitiful.

It was dreadful how much Emma liked her.

"Mr. Coleman is a good man, and he is very deserving of this beautiful castle," Miss Fitzroy said in a polite voice. "You are fortunate to have been his friend all these years. I fear we have not had the chance to become as acquainted as we should be considering our..." she lowered her voice, "upcoming union." Miss Fitzroy knew that Emma was aware of the engagement, but that the gentlemen were not. She must have understood the wisdom in keeping it a secret to secure their investments. Two gentlemen, Mr. Dudley and Lord Watlington, had already joined them at the table for breakfast. With Miss Fitzroy present, and seemingly unattached, the men were now focused on her as they ate in silence. It was a welcome relief to not be the only young woman present. The bruise on Mr. Dudley's forehead was almost gone, but the outline of yellow and green was still visible even from across the table. Lord Watlington would likely soon be asking Miss Fitzroy about her opinion on reptiles. Lady Burgess and Mrs. Coleman, who had become fast friends, conversed loudly at the other end of the table while Emma and Miss Fitzroy spoke.

Guilt drove deeper into Emma's chest. How could Harry destroy Miss Fitzroy's hopes in such a way? It warmed Emma's heart each time she thought of how determined Harry now was to choose her, but she couldn't rid herself of the shame of it. She had always felt that Miss Fitzroy had stolen Harry from her, but now she was beginning to feel the opposite.

"You must tell me as much as you can about Mr. Coleman," Miss Fitzroy said with a smile.

"Oh, there is not much to tell." Emma shifted in her chair. Would it help Miss Fitzroy endure her loss more if Emma made Harry sound less wonderful than he truly was? "Mr. Coleman is as ordinary as any man can be, but perhaps slightly more agreeable than the average gentleman." She took a quick bite of bread from her plate, hoping to avoid speaking further.

Miss Fitzroy's dark eyes shifted toward the door as Harry walked through it, followed by Mr. Seaton.

Emma's eyes connected with Harry's instantly, so she

hurried to look down at her plate. As he walked toward the sideboard where the food had been set out, she stole another glance at him, even though it had been her idea not to stare at him during breakfast. Her heart raced. She hoped he would speak to Miss Fitzroy sooner rather than later, but she also hoped to be far away from Mrs. Coleman when it happened. Harry looked just as nervous as he walked back to the table, taking the chair on Miss Fitzroy's other side. Her posture straightened as he sat down, and Emma strained her ears to overhear their conversation. Harry did not waste any time.

"Miss Fitzroy, I wondered if you might be willing to linger in the dining room when the other guests have finished eating. There is a matter I wish to discuss privately with you."

Emma slid her gaze carefully in Miss Fitzroy's direction to observe her reaction. Her heart hammered with renewed guilt at the look of concern on Miss Fitzroy's profile. "Of course."

Emma snapped her gaze back to her plate. At least it would all be over with after breakfast. Emma could hardly eat another bite with the upset state of her stomach, so she sipped from her water cup instead. Some of the guests had barely started eating, and not everyone had even arrived. She frowned. Where was Mr. Hale? Was he missing again? Just as the thought crossed her mind, the door opened at the hands of the footman, and Mr. Hale walked into the room. There was something different in his posture—a lack of confidence that Emma hadn't seen before. His mouth was firm, his gaze cast down as he came closer to the table.

Emma continued to observe him as he finally looked up, his eyes settling on Miss Fitzroy.

Lady Burgess's loud voice had been prattling on about some gossip she had heard in London, but it stopped abruptly, leaving the room much more silent than it had been before. She was staring at Mr. Hale, a look of unmasked dismay dawning on her face.

Miss Fitzroy blanched, her shoulder blades pinching together. Her fork dropped to the table, and she hurried to pick it up. Emma watched the growing signs of alarm in her features for a long moment before Mrs. Coleman, apparently oblivious to it all, stood from the table. "Ah, Mr. Hale, we missed you at dinner yesterday evening. Have you met our new guests, Lady Burgess and Miss Fitzroy?"

Mr. Hale seemed to have been hoping to sneak to the sideboard unnoticed, but he turned to face Mrs. Coleman. A muscle jumped in his jaw, and he pushed a strand of auburn hair behind his ear nervously. "Yes, we have already been acquainted." He gave a bow in Miss Fitzroy's direction without meeting her gaze, then to Lady Burgess, who was eyeing him with enough malice to make Emma squirm in her seat. There was no fondness between them, that much was certain.

"Is that so?" Mrs. Coleman gasped, smiling in Mr. Hale's direction. "How did you become acquainted with these ladies?"

Mr. Hale gathered his thoughts for a moment. "In Devon, ma'am. I spent last summer there with my grandfather."

"What a fortunate coincidence." Mrs. Coleman's smile

faltered when she seemed to notice the daggers in Lady Burgess's eyes for the first time.

Mr. Hale cleared his throat, crossing his arms over his chest. He looked stranded in the middle of the room, as if he didn't know what to say or do or even where to look. He kept his gaze fixed on Mrs. Coleman. "And how are you acquainted with Lady Burgess and Miss Fitzroy?"

Before Mrs. Coleman could give whatever rehearsed answer she had that didn't involve the engagement, Lady Burgess leaned forward in her chair, lifting her sharp chin. "My daughter is engaged to marry Mr. Coleman."

Mrs. Coleman's eyes widened at the revelation of that secret, her lips pinching together.

Harry muttered something under his breath.

Mr. Hale stared at Miss Fitzroy, then at Harry, his eyes heavy with surprise. Miss Fitzroy refused to look at him. She looked on the verge of tears.

After a long moment of stunned silence, Mr. Hale spoke again, his voice firm. "I offer my congratulations to you both."

"How long have you been engaged, Mr. Coleman?" Mr. Dudley asked in his nasally voice, his mouth half full of eggs. "It seems the sort of happy news that would not have been kept in such confidence."

Could this be any more disastrous? Emma couldn't see Harry from where she sat, but she sensed his discontent as much as she felt her own. Lord Watlington and Mr. Seaton were listening for his answer as well. She prayed he wouldn't denounce the engagement in front of everyone, and thankfully he was too kind to do that to Miss Fitzroy.

"A few months," he said in a weak voice.

Mr. Dudley whispered something to Lord Watlington before they both turned their attention back to their plates. Mr. Hale remained stranded between the table and sideboard, his features tight against whatever emotion he was hiding. In an instant, Miss Fitzroy stood from the table, her chair screeching against the floor.

"Please excuse me," she said before hurrying toward the door. Her face was red, her hands balled into fists at her sides.

Harry stood, attempting to follow her, but she whirled around and held up a hand. "Please. I—I only need a breath of air." She gave a smile before rushing away, leaving Harry standing alone near the door. He returned to his chair in silence.

"Well." Mrs. Coleman gave a nervous chuckle, dabbing at her lips with her serviette. "Has everyone enjoyed the ham? I think it is particularly flavorful today."

"Very delicious," Mr. Dudley said after a swallow.

With an empty chair between Emma and Harry, she now had a clear view of his face. He met her concerned gaze. They couldn't speak their thoughts aloud with so many other people nearby, but the tension in the room was obvious. Whatever stir Mr. Hale had caused was lingering in the air, and Lady Burgess hadn't ceased glaring at him. "Please excuse my daughter's hasty departure, Mr. Coleman," Lady Burgess said, turning toward Harry with an apologetic look. It was mingled with panic. "She-she did not sleep well during our long journey and I suspect she has a headache."

Emma's mind spun. It was clear that Miss Fitzroy's unfit condition had been caused by Mr. Hale, nothing else. The moment Miss Fitzroy had seen him, her face had turned a ghostly white. If Harry could not speak with her alone at that moment, it didn't mean Emma couldn't. If she excused herself from the room, no one would suspect she was going to find Miss Fitzroy. They were barely acquainted.

She offered her plate to a footman to clear away and then stood. "Excuse me," she said with a smile before starting toward the door. She felt Harry's gaze follow her out. She felt guilty abandoning him to the awkwardness in the dining room, but she needed to discover what had distressed Miss Fitzroy so greatly. Had it been entirely Mr. Hale's entrance, or had it been that her mother had announced her engagement?

She turned the corner toward the staircase, but stopped when she heard the sound of labored breathing. Miss Fitzroy was standing in the dark corridor ahead, her face in her hands. She took a deep breath, pacing in a circle.

"Miss Fitzroy?" Emma's voice echoed.

She jerked around, her hand flying to her chest. "Miss Eastwood. You frightened me." She hastily wiped at her cheek, but Emma noticed.

Emma walked forward with slow steps. "Forgive me for presuming that you would confide in me on such a short acquaintance, but I came to ask what distresses you. I-I noticed the effect Mr. Hale's entrance had on you."

Miss Fitzroy's guarded expression melted, and she tipped her head back. "Was it so obvious? Oh, what he must think of me." She sniffed, shaking her head with a groan.

"He seemed just as surprised to see you."

Miss Fitzroy nodded. "And even more surprised to find that I am engaged to Mr. Coleman." She wiped at another tear on her face, her hand shaking.

What could have happened between Miss Fitzroy and Mr. Hale to be causing her such unrest? She seemed hardly able to collect her thoughts or compose herself. Emma empathized with the feeling. Only strong emotions could cause such a reaction.

Miss Fitzroy took a steadying breath. "I don't suspect he will stay long at Garsley now. At least I might not have to face him again."

"What happened between the two of you?" Emma asked in a gentle voice. When Emma was emotional, she was more inclined to keep her feelings a secret, but Miss Fitzroy seemed as if she might benefit from sharing. She seemed near to bursting with the burden of it all.

"My elder brother, who has already inherited my father's title, and my mother, have always hoped for me to make an advantageous match with my dowry. Last summer, Mr. Hale came to my neighborhood to visit his grandfather. At the time of his visit, Mr. Hale was not wealthy. He and his family were unheard of." Miss Fitzroy sniffed, rubbing her nose. "But I came to know him, and we began meeting in secret. I fell in love with him." She gulped. "We knew my brother and mother would not approve of the match, so we planned to elope. On the night of our planned elopement, we were discovered and our carriage was stopped by my brother.

"He accused Mr. Hale of being a fortune hunter, of destroying my honor, and challenged him to a duel. During that duel, the wounds Mr. Hale inflicted on my brother with his sword were nearly fatal." Her wide eyes blinked fast. "He was defending his own life, so I do not blame him." She sighed. "But my family convinced me of the error in my choice, and I felt that I had no choice but to never see Mr. Hale again. And I hadn't seen him until today." She caught her breath. "I broke his heart. I didn't know what to do. How could I have married him after such a horrible incident? I didn't know at the time that my brother would recover. Being married to the man who killed him would not have been possible. To this day, my brother still speaks of him with hatred. As does my mother."

Emma's mind reeled. She remembered Mr. Hale's refusal to participate in the fencing tournament, and how he had claimed to have seen the darker side of the activity. She never would have predicted that sort of history. "Does Mr. Hale know that your brother survived the wounds?"

Miss Fitzroy shook her head. "I don't know how he would."

"You must tell him. It would put his guilt at ease. It might even give him reason to hope that you could be together again."

A tear slipped down Miss Fitzroy's cheek. "My mother despises him. She would never approve."

"Do you still love him?" Emma asked in a hushed voice.

Miss Fitzroy nodded as she rubbed her nose again. "I have never stopped."

Emma's heart pounded. "Then it isn't too late. Perhaps you were meant to be reunited."

Miss Fitzroy's shoulders stiffened, a trace of panic overtaking her features. "I should not have told you any of this. Please do not repeat these words. I am engaged to Mr. Coleman. I cannot face Mr. Hale." She shook her head fast.

"If you still love him, you must!" Emma couldn't allow Mr. Hale to leave Garsley until he and Miss Fitzroy had spoken. What if they could be together again? Desperation clung to her. Emma had felt like the reason so many things had been ruined. What if she could help repair the broken relationship between Miss Fitzroy and Mr. Hale? The chances of them both being at Garsley were so slight. There was a reason they were both there at the same time. If Miss Fitzroy could make amends with Mr. Hale, then Emma wouldn't feel nearly as horrible about the engagement ending.

"I cannot," Miss Fitzroy said. "I will keep my distance until he leaves."

"Won't you regret not having one conversation with him? You might discover that his feelings too are unchanged."

"And then what?" Miss Fitzroy asked in a shaky voice. "Mr. Coleman's entire plan for his hotel is depending on my dowry."

It wasn't Emma's place to tell her that Harry had reconsidered, so she thought carefully about what to say. "Isn't your entire future depending on your decision of who you spend it with? You must ensure you are making the right choice."

Miss Fitzroy's wide brown eyes grew still, her tears ceasing.

"If you would like, I will speak to Mr. Hale," Emma offered. "He has become my friend during his time here, so he might confide in me about his feelings." Calling him her friend was a bit of an exaggeration, but he had spoken to her about how he had been hurt by love before—by Miss Fitzroy. The coincidence was astonishing, but also very opportune. And fateful. They could not waste this chance.

Miss Fitzroy wrung her fingers together. "That would put me at ease, I suppose, to know a few of his thoughts prior to attempting a private conversation with him." She pressed a hand to her belly as she took a deep breath. "I have never been more nervous."

"I will speak with him today," Emma said.

"He will likely be leaving now that he has seen me," Miss Fitzroy said with a sniff.

"I will do all I can to convince him to stay."

The sound of footfalls came from around the corner. "Daphne?" The female voice hissed in a whisper. It must have been Lady Burgess.

Miss Fitzroy backed away. "I must go."

Emma nodded as Miss Fitzroy scurried down the corridor and out of sight before her mother rounded the corner. Lady Burgess squinted as she approached Emma, her thick ringlets swaying in time with her blue taffeta skirts. "Miss Eastwood, have you seen my daughter?"

"I'm afraid not." Before she could be questioned further, she slipped past Lady Burgess with a curtsy.

Her heart thudded. She could hardly wait to tell Harry what she had just discovered. He might not have to be the cause of the broken engagement after all. If it became Miss Fitzroy's decision, then Harry could still be true to his word. Mrs. Coleman might accept Emma as her future daughter-in-law. There was no longer any reason to be hasty. Emma had some matchmaking to do.

CHAPTER TWENTY

Emma waited in an alcove in the corridor outside the breakfast room until she saw Harry walk out the door. He started in her direction, and as he passed, she whispered his name. "Harry!"

He jumped, cursing under his breath.

Emma couldn't stop the laugh that bubbled out of her chest. She waved him forward, grabbing him by the arm when he was close enough.

"Is this some sort of revenge?" he asked, his features still recovering from the shock.

"You deserve it after startling me out of my wits last night."

A smile lingered on his mouth, but his eyes were weary. His plan to speak with Miss Fitzroy after breakfast had failed when she fled the room and her mother announced the engagement to all the guests. He must have been frustrated and feeling the pressure of the task at hand.

Emma could hardly wait to tell him what she had just discovered.

She planned her next words in her head, but she couldn't concentrate with him standing so close. His brown eyes were partially hooded by his lashes as they traced over her face. He seemed to have lost a bit of concentration too. It was difficult for Emma to suppress the happiness she felt knowing that Harry loved her. With so many obstacles still to overcome, she had momentarily forgotten how completely unexpected it was. He wanted her. He had made that clear, and he was still making that clear by the way he was looking at her.

"I followed Miss Fitzroy," she whispered, shaking herself free of Harry's distractions. "I found it strange how unsettled she seemed by Mr. Hale."

Harry's eyes widened. "Did you speak with her?"

Emma gave an eager nod. She relayed all the details of Miss Fitzroy's past with Mr. Hale. When she finished, Harry rubbed his hand over his face, letting out a slow breath. "Does she still love him?"

"She does."

He shook his head in astonishment, relief washing over his expression. "We cannot allow him to leave."

"Leave?"

"Just now, before he left the breakfast room, he told me of his plans to leave today without any further explanation. He must feel obligated to leave in order to prevent further distress to Miss Fitzroy. He also believes that she is going to marry me…so that news could not have been easy for him to endure."

Emma's heart leaped. "No! He must stay for long enough to speak with her."

Harry gave an amused smile, and he touched her face softly with his thumb. "Are we to conspire a matchmaking scheme together?" A shiver raced after his touch, all the way down her neck and shoulders.

"It seems we must." She smiled, her pulse racing. "Miss Fitzroy and Mr. Hale deserve to be happy together. You may not have to break off the engagement after all. I will speak to Mr. Hale today before he leaves. I will do as I did for Miss Fitzroy—encourage him to follow his heart."

"There are many forces against them being together," Harry warned. "Perhaps if I break off the engagement first, Mr. Hale will feel more free to pursue her again."

"If you break off the engagement, Miss Fitzroy will surely leave Garsley at once. We must give it time. Mr. Hale doesn't know that her brother survived his wounds. That will give him hope."

"Do you truly think it will? Even after causing *injury* to her brother? He is hated by her entire family."

"And I am hated by yours," Emma muttered.

"My mother doesn't hate you." There was a laugh behind the words, but he didn't know how Mrs. Coleman had practically barged into Emma's room to tell her to leave Garsley and what little she thought of her. Emma's heart clenched with a familiar ache. In a small way, she felt empathy for Mr. Hale. She, too, had been tempted to run away.

A set of footfalls met her ears from down the corridor. Emma's spine stiffened, and she backed farther into the alcove.

Mrs. Coleman's voice echoed. "Harry?"

Emma was still not completely out of sight. If Mrs. Coleman came any closer, she would be easily seen. There was nothing to obstruct Emma from her view but Harry and his broad shoulders.

The footfalls continued, and soon Mrs. Coleman was standing directly in front of them. Her eyes fell on Emma, and her features darkened instantly. Her nose twitched.

"Mother." Harry stepped away from Emma, an innocent smile on his face.

Mrs. Coleman interlocked her hands, her shoulders stiffening. "What were the two of you discussing in such a secretive manner?"

"We are worried for Miss Fitzroy," Harry said. His voice was surprisingly calm. "She seems unwell."

"Lady Burgess has gone to look for her." Mrs. Coleman's suspicious gaze still flickered back to Emma repeatedly. "As her betrothed, *you* should be expressing similar concern to her."

"She wished to be alone."

Mrs. Coleman huffed a breath, crossing her arms and planting her feet. She was obviously not planning on leaving Harry and Emma alone together again. Discussing their plan would be difficult, but the first step was already quite clear to Emma. She needed to find Mr. Hale and encourage him to stay. If he knew Miss Fitzroy still loved him, it might be enough to change his mind. It had been enough for Harry and Emma.

"Please excuse me," Emma said with a quick curtsy. It pained her to surrender under Mrs. Coleman's sharp gaze, but her departure was necessary in that instance. She needed to catch Mr. Hale before he had a chance to leave.

She knew his room was on the third floor, so she started in that direction first. She passed Mr. Dudley on the staircase, offering a curtsy before continuing up to the third floor corridor. The walls were lined with portraits of the previous families who had occupied the castle, the gold frames illuminated by the window at the end of the corridor. She didn't know what exactly she planned to do. She couldn't very well knock on his door. She hesitated, walking the length of the corridor and studying the portraits on the wall. After a few minutes, a young male servant walked up the staircase. Emma stopped him.

"Pardon me, but may I ask who has called for you?"

The young man's blue eyes rounded in bewilderment. "'tis Mr. Hale, miss. I'm 'is valet." He gave a quick bow.

"Will you please tell him that I wish to speak with him?"

The young man nodded, hurrying off in the direction of Mr. Hale's room. Shortly after he disappeared inside, the door opened again, and Mr. Hale stepped out. His creased brow looked just as it had that morning at breakfast.

"Miss Eastwood?" He gave a bow, his confusion obvious when he met her gaze. "How may I be of service?"

"I heard that you planned to leave." She tested him with a tilt of her head. "Is that true?"

Mr. Hale sighed, his jaw tightening. "It is. Unfortunately I must hide from the new guests in a more...permanent fashion." He gave a painful smile. "If you could not see from her behavior in the dining room, Lady Burgess is not fond of me."

Emma chose her words carefully. "But Miss Fitzroy is fond of you."

Mr. Hale froze, his eyes lifting to Emma's. "How did you reach that conclusion?"

"I spoke with her," Emma relented. "She told me everything about your history. You need not hide it from me. She also told me that she regrets not marrying you against her family's wishes, and that she still loves you." Emma spoke in as gentle a voice as she could manage. The hope in Mr. Hale's eyes was delicate, a show of emotion she rarely saw from him.

It faded quickly, a shaky exhale escaping his chest. "It doesn't matter. She is engaged to Mr. Coleman. It makes sense. She was always ambitious. Far too ambitious to end up married to me." His nostrils flared. "I put my feelings to rest long ago. I had to. I can't have hope of marrying a woman whose brother died at my hands." His eyes flooded with guilt, and he looked at the floor as if to hide it.

"He didn't die," Emma said in a quick voice. "He recovered. Miss Fitzroy confirmed it herself."

Mr. Hale looked up, that glimmer of hope rising again on his face. "Did he?" he breathed. "I never received word. I assumed the worst."

"There is still hope for you to be reconciled with the family." Emma paused, fiddling with a loose thread on her skirts. "Do you still love her?" She held her breath.

Mr. Hale sighed. "Does it matter? She is marrying Mr. Coleman." His features bore the weight of his heartache. Though he hadn't admitted his feelings, they were written all over his face.

"She may not be," Emma whispered. She leaned closer.

"If you will confide in me, I will confide in you. Can I trust you?"

"Of course." Mr. Hale frowned.

Emma pressed her lips together. "You were not wrong in your suspicions about the existence of...certain feelings between Harry and me." She scolded herself for blushing at the confession. "He planned to break off the engagement before Miss Fitzroy arrived, but then she came sooner than expected. He has been waiting for the right moment to tell her, but now that we know this history between you...we thought it prudent to wait to see if there is any hope for the two of you to be together."

She studied his face. She had clearly overwhelmed him, but she took it as a good sign. "Her family would never support the match," he said. "Despite the fortune I have gained, and her brother's survival, I still dueled him. I still wounded him."

"If you and Miss Fitzroy love each other, that is reason enough to marry anyway."

"It is not." Mr. Hale's eyes flashed with frustration. "It wasn't enough before. It isn't enough now. There are some obstacles too great to be overcome by love. It may very well work for you and Mr. Coleman, but Miss Fitzroy's mother will be determined to stop any union from forming between us."

Emma bit her lip, her mind racing. "I invite you to speak with Miss Fitzroy before making any hasty decision to leave. There is no pain worse than regret. If during that meeting you find that you cannot part from her again, Harry and I are prepared to assist you in a successful elopement if that is necessary." Her heart pounded as she said the words. Harry hadn't confirmed his desire to be involved in such a scheme, but she had volunteered him nonetheless.

Mr. Hale was silent, his face paler than it had been at the beginning of their conversation. "How can this meeting take place? Knowing I'm here, I highly doubt her mother will leave her side."

Emma squared her shoulders, her determination building until she was near to bursting. "If you are available, plan to meet her inside the keep at three o'clock this afternoon." That was the time Mrs. Coleman took tea, and she would surely invite Lady Burgess and Miss Fitzroy, who could pretend to be too unwell to go. "You may leave the rest of the details to me."

CHAPTER TWENTY-ONE

"What am I to do?" Miss Fitzroy paced in a circle on the grass, her dark curls lifting from her forehead with the breeze. She pressed a hand to her heart, her breathing quick and labored. "He loves me."

Emma grinned. "Marry him! That's what you are to do."

Miss Fitzroy had just left her meeting with Mr. Hale in the keep. Emma had been standing outside, watching to ensure they were not interrupted. After waiting in the cold for nearly an hour, she had been eager to speak to Miss Fitzroy about the result of their private conversation. Emma's nose and hands were numb as she awaited more of the details. Harry had known about the meeting, and had been doing all he could to entertain Mr. Dudley, Mr. Seaton, and Lord Watlington to ensure they didn't step outside and witness anything suspicious, and to ensure Lady Burgess and his mother didn't end their tea earlier than expected.

Miss Fitzroy had emerged from the keep with Mr. Hale,

both of their faces bright with smiles of relief and giddiness. Emma had never seen such an expression on Mr. Hale's face, but it warmed her heart. Mr. Hale had gone back inside to avoid suspicion, and now Miss Fitzroy glanced in both directions, as if she and Emma might be overheard. She continued her pacing. "On one hand, I am happier than I have ever been at the thought of marrying Mr. Hale, but on the other, I feel like the worst of all women to break off an engagement to a respectable man like Mr. Coleman." She bit her fingernail.

Had Mr. Hale not told her about Harry's wishes to break off the engagement? About his attachment to Emma? He might not have felt that it was his place to do so. She swallowed, considering the best way to proceed. "Your desire to break off the engagement will not come as a surprise to Mr. Coleman."

Miss Fitzroy's brows shot up. "What do you mean?"

"I hope you will not be upset with me, but I told him the history between you and Mr. Hale. And..." she took a deep breath. "It so happens that I have a history of my own with Mr. Coleman."

Miss Fitzroy's jaw lowered slightly, a dazed smile tugging at the corners. "Do continue."

"We recently confessed our feelings for one another." Emma covered half her face with her hand. "As it happens, he has been meaning to end the engagement himself. When I learned of your love for Mr. Hale, we hoped you would find hope to marry him and a mutual desire to end the engagement."

Miss Fitzroy's eyes were round, her lips still parted. And

then a laugh burst out of her, and she slapped a hand over her mouth. "How can it be so easy?"

Emma would not call it *easy* by any means. But after months of pining after Mr. Hale, perhaps it did feel easy to Miss Fitzroy. After years of pining after Harry, Emma hadn't dared to dream it would come to this. Her eyes stung. Falling in love was easy, but finding her way to Harry hadn't been.

But it wasn't over yet. There was still one remaining obstacle.

Mrs. Coleman.

Emma could still feel the disdain and judgment in her gaze when she had found Harry speaking with Emma in the corridor. They would have to take more care. Until Mr. Hale and Miss Fitzroy were successfully on their way to Gretna Green, the engagement officially broken off with no hope of being renewed, Mrs. Coleman and Lady Burgess needed to remain ignorant.

Miss Fitzroy lowered her voice. "I will speak to Harry before dinner. If what you say is true, then we will reach an agreement to break off our engagement without any trouble." Her face broke into a smile, her flushed lips stretching wide. "Oh, Miss Eastwood. We shall both be happy." She squeezed her hand. "Thank you."

"You must still pretend to be engaged until the elopement takes place," Emma said. "As far as your mother and Mrs. Coleman are concerned, your standing engagement can act as a cover for your elopement. After that, we shall both be free to marry for love."

Freedom was a strange concept, but Emma clung to it as she and Miss Fitzroy sneaked back into the castle.

Emma felt the edge of her fork digging into her hand. The tension at the dining table was thick enough to slice in two, and if she continued to hold her fork so tightly, the same would happen to her fingers. She loosened her grip, meeting Harry's gaze against her better judgment. She hadn't had a moment to speak with him alone. Had Miss Fitzroy followed through on her plan to break off the engagement that afternoon? Or had she changed her mind?

There was no way of knowing simply by looking at Harry's face.

He was unreadable.

Either Miss Fitzroy hadn't spoken with him as she had promised, or Harry was becoming a very skilled actor.

Mr. Hale had opted to take his meal in his room again. His avoidance of Lady Burgess was for the best. Their last encounter had been too awkward to repeat, especially with an audience. It was better to let Lady Burgess think that Mr. Hale was planning to leave Garsley soon and never return. She wouldn't have to see him again—at least not until after her daughter married him and she had no choice. Was it horrible to help such a scheme take place? Emma immediately suppressed the thought. Miss Fitzroy seemed to think that her mother would never support her marriage to Mr. Hale, so waiting until a later time would do nothing to persuade her. Miss Fitzroy was nearly thirty years old. She could make decisions for herself.

The visiting bachelors had yet to be informed that there would be nothing to invest in, but Emma doubted they would be nearly as disappointed as Mrs. Coleman and Lady

Burgess when the truth came crumbling down on them. Emma could envision them leaving happily enough knowing that they were able to spend several weeks in a place so grand with food such as the meal they were eating that evening.

Although the dessert meringues were delicious, Emma had no appetite. She took one bite before her stomach twisted, much like it had with the other courses of the meal.

Emma caught Miss Fitzroy's gaze from across the table as her mother began speaking of the wedding again. If she looked content—and a little proud—did that mean she had broken off the engagement? There was no worry in her expression, only certainty and politeness.

Emma's foot tapped faster on the floor under the table.

The drawing room activities dragged on for far too long, and when Emma was asked to sing for the guests, Lady Burgess said, "Oh, Miss Eastwood, please tell us you will stay for long enough to sing for the guests at the wedding as well."

Emma declined as kindly as she could, exercising all her restraint not to look at Harry where she knew he sat all the way across the room. Would she even discover the answers to her questions that evening? Or would she have to wait until the next day? She wouldn't sleep that night, she was sure of it.

Miss Fitzroy and Lady Burgess retired first. Emma watched them go, her hope of speaking with Miss Fitzroy alone withering away before her eyes. The dim candlelight flickered on the faces of the remaining guests. Mr. Dudley with his book in the corner, Mr. Seaton, who had chosen the seat beside Emma, and Mr. Watlington who would likely soon excuse himself.

Mrs. Coleman was sitting on the settee. Her spine was straight, and she had nothing to occupy her but the observation of the others in the room.

Harry's dark hair fell over his forehead as he looked down at his book, the line of his jaw sharp in the shadows. In an instant, the book snapped shut, and he stood. "Good evening, everyone." He gave a bow, his eyes slipping toward Emma momentarily. For the first time all evening, a flash of emotion crossed his face.

The dimple dented his cheek as he smiled.

Emma's heart picked up speed. The smile was only meant for her, because it vanished as he walked past his mother and exited the room. Emma wanted to follow him immediately, but she knew better. She would be left wondering what that smile meant all night. How could she bear it? She had never been more curious.

After waiting a reasonable amount of time—ten minutes by her estimation—she excused herself as well, eager to leave the reaches of Mrs. Coleman's watchful eye. She hurried down the corridor, a frown etched on her brow. If Miss Fitzroy was in good spirits and Harry was smiling, then the engagement was off, wasn't it?

She could safely assume so, could she not?

She bit her lower lip as her feet carried her quickly away from the drawing room. As she walked past the study, she noticed a flicker of candlelight underneath the door, and then it opened.

She hardly had time to catch sight of Harry before he grabbed her arm and tugged her inside.

She tripped forward, a surprised gasp catching in her throat. "Harry—"

He closed the door behind her, his hand reaching for the latch between her arm and her waist. Once it was secure, his hand pressed into her lower back and he pulled her close. His smile came into view, the dimple in his cheek—the warmth of his brown eyes behind his spectacles. "The engagement is off."

Emma's heart raced, a wave of relief washing over her skin. The elation that followed was strong enough to make her balance falter. A small part of her couldn't comprehend it. Harry was free. He was hers. "Are you being serious?" She gave a laugh of disbelief, but it was cut off by Harry's lips.

His kiss lingered for several seconds, and she breathed him in, her lungs swelling in her chest as his arms wrapped around her.

When he pulled back, her vision was hazy. "I have never been more so," he whispered. His expression was equal parts playful and intense, the raw adoration in his eyes jerking her forward like a team of horses under a whip. "Is it too presumptuous to ask if you'll marry me instead?" he whispered.

"Far too presumptuous." She smiled without reservation, her throat tight as she pulled him back to her by the front of his waistcoat.

She had thought his kisses had been breathtaking before, but this was different. There was even more certainty in the way his lips moved over hers, the tightness with which he held her against him. His fingertips against her back were the only anchor she had with reality. Harry was kissing her. He wanted to marry her. All the years of dreaming, of hoping, of wishing for a moment like the one she had now—they were worth it. Her heart was on fire. The thrill racing across her skin was moving too quickly to keep up with, so she melted into the motion of Harry's touches and kisses instead, momentarily forgetting to breathe.

She rose on her toes, wrapping her arms around his neck, and his arms tightened around her waist. The weightlessness she felt wasn't only in her mind—he had lifted her off the floor. His spectacles slid down his nose, falling against her face. They both laughed as her feet touched the floor again.

"Why are you wearing those horrible things?" Emma teased, her voice weak just like the rest of her.

Harry's laugh sent a pulse of warmth through her body. He removed the spectacles and tossed them onto the desk behind her. Then he gripped her waist tighter and hoisted her up to the desk just the same. A light gasp escaped her throat as he kissed her again, his hands settling at the top of her hips. She was likely crushing the old hotel plans that were sitting on the desk, but her heart soared at the reminder that Harry no longer cared. He had chosen her instead. She felt his lips curl into a smile, his eyes meeting hers briefly before he pressed a trail of kisses over her neck, firm at first, then soft, a playful combination that left her breathless.

This was a side of Harry she had never imagined, but it might have been her favorite so far.

Just when his mouth found hers again, a firm knock sounded on the door.

She met his eyes with panic, scurrying off the desk as he released her waist.

"Harry?" Mrs. Coleman's voice came through the door.

"One moment." Harry said, his voice surprisingly nonchalant. He searched the room, but Emma had already started toward the window. The heavy blue drapes would cover her sufficiently—at least she hoped so. Being caught in Harry's study behind a locked door was not the way to announce their love to Harry's mother. They needed to keep it secret for long enough to allow Mr. Hale and Miss Fitzroy their escape. Emma slid behind the drapes and Harry arranged them until she was hidden completely.

She listened to his footfalls as he crossed the room. Her pulse had already been quick before, but now it raced to a dangerous level. She pressed a hand to her chest, struggling to slow her breathing. If Mrs. Coleman detected her there, she would be mortified. The backside of the drapes smelled of dust and mildew. It reminded her of Mr. Blyth.

Emma listened as the latch slid open and the door hinges creaked. Then came Harry's voice. "Mother."

A rustle of skirts came into the room. "What are you still doing awake?" Mrs. Coleman asked in an accusatory voice.

"Nothing of consequence." There was an edge of confusion in Harry's tone.

Mrs. Coleman sighed. "I have just finished speaking with Lady Burgess. She has informed me of a most disconcerting history between Miss Fitzroy and Mr. Hale."

"I have been informed," Harry said.

"Well? Why have you done nothing about it?" Mrs. Coleman's voice was shrill. "Mr. Hale must be sent away. He has had the audacity to stay far too long already considering the circumstances. How could he burden Lady Burgess with his presence here after he nearly murdered her son?" Mrs. Coleman's voice shook. "And he is not the only one overstaying his welcome."

The longcase clock near the window ticked three times before Harry spoke. "Shall I send all the gentlemen away? Will that satisfy you?"

"I'm not speaking of the other gentlemen. I'm speaking of Miss Eastwood. I suspect her presence here is troubling Miss Fitzroy."

"Miss Fitzroy did not seem the least bit troubled this evening. She was in good spirits."

"It is time for Miss Eastwood to leave. She failed to attract a husband, and the time we gave her was generous. Lady Burgess has had many questions about Miss Eastwood and her relationship with you, and she has looked upon it with no small measure of suspicion."

"Miss Eastwood will stay for as long as she wishes."

Mrs. Coleman scoffed. "You cannot possibly plan to have her stay here even after you are married."

"I do plan on that, actually."

Mrs. Coleman grunted in frustration. "Miss Fitzroy will not approve."

"On the contrary, I think she will. She is very understanding, and she and Emma have become swift friends."

"I think Miss Eastwood is plotting something."

Harry fell silent again, and Emma listened to her own heartbeat in her ears for several seconds.

"What might she be plotting?" Harry asked in a skeptical tone.

"I think she is trying to bring Mr. Hale and Miss Fitzroy together again," Mrs. Coleman hissed. "She has been sneaking around, and I will not stand for it. Neither should you. I have not forgotten how the two of you were hiding in the shadows of the corridor in some...secret conversation. If you lose Miss Fitzroy, we lose the hotel. You have not been doing enough to impress her. I have hardly seen the two of you interacting."

"Mother." Harry's voice was firm, stopping Mrs. Coleman's rambling. "If Miss Fitzroy chooses not to marry me, then Emma is not the one to blame."

"Do you have reason to believe that Miss Fitzroy won't marry you?" Mrs. Coleman seemed on the brink of combustion, her voice a high squeak.

Emma waited, holding her breath. Would Harry keep it a secret? Or would he tell her the truth right then? If Lady Burgess was informed, she would lead her daughter away from Garsley immediately, ruining Miss Fitzroy's chance to elope.

"No," Harry answered.

Emma released her breath slowly, keeping as quiet as she could behind the curtain.

"Then why does she seem hesitant when the subject of your wedding is brought up?" Mrs. Coleman's skirts rustled again. "Why do *you* seem hesitant? Does Miss Fitzroy sense that your affections are elsewhere?"

"I don't know what you mean," Harry said.

"Answer one more question, and I will put the subject to rest." Mrs. Coleman's final question rang through the air. "Have you fallen in love with Miss Eastwood?"

Lie again, Emma demanded in her mind. She wouldn't be hurt; she would know he was lying. She waited, dread pouring through her as the seconds ticked on with no answer.

"Would it matter to you if I had?" Harry asked, his voice tight with anger. "All you want is the hotel. My happiness is secondary."

"Harry!" His mother growled. "Tell me at once."

"It is late, Mother. Please excuse me. I have work to finish."

Emma could sense Mrs. Coleman's rage without even seeing her face. "I *knew* I never should have allowed her to stay here," she said. "I *knew* she was a seductress from the moment I saw her and learned who her mother was."

"Do not speak of her with so little respect."

"How shall I respect a woman who does nothing to deserve it? I know what happened between Miss Eastwood and Sir Francis. I know of her attempts to seduce him."

"That is not what happened." Harry's voice wavered with his own anger.

"I invite you to think on the wisdom of allowing such a woman to distract you from your dream. Her being here has put me ill at ease from the beginning."

"I think it is *you* who has put Miss Eastwood ill at ease," Harry said. "She has been kind and gracious, and all you have done is made her feel unwelcome and ashamed of who she is. *I love* who she is, and I would not change a single thing."

Emma squeezed her eyes shut. His words flooded her cheeks with warmth, but dread followed them just as quickly. He was not doing his part to keep his mother's suspicion at bay. He was feeding it.

A dismayed gasp came from Mrs. Coleman.

"Goodnight, Mother." Harry must have ushered her out the door, because the last sound Emma heard was his mother's sputtering search for words and then the click of the door and screech of the latch.

A few seconds later, Harry walked toward the window, pulling aside the drapes. He looked at her like a child who had just been caught stealing biscuits from the kitchen.

"Harry!" Emma whispered. "Now she is even more suspicious!"

"I couldn't deny my feelings." He shook his head, his jaw tight. "She wants to control everything, but this she cannot."

Emma sighed, her heart aching from the cruelty of Mrs. Coleman's words. She tried not to allow them to affect her, but they had still managed to make a home in her chest. Mrs. Coleman was the new Arabella. How could Emma live the rest of her life knowing that her mother-in-law wanted her gone? That she resented her?

Even though those questions plagued her, the alternative of living her life without Harry sounded much worse. His eyes gazed into hers, his brows drawn together. He must have sensed her thoughts, because he said, "she is wrong about you. Entirely wrong, and we will prove it to her. Once she knows you, I promise she will be unable to help herself from loving you. It's impossible not to."

Emma scoffed, her throat becoming raw. "Mr. Dudley did not love me when I nearly split his head open."

Harry tipped his head back with a laugh. "Of that I'm glad. I was ill-tempered enough with the other bachelors doting on you. I was glad to have one less to vex me."

Emma smiled, her heart growing lighter by the second. Harry had a way of doing that.

"My mother will come to her senses," he said. "Once

Miss Fitzroy and Mr. Hale are gone along with all hope of the hotel, she will eventually learn to love and forgive me again, and I'm sure she will also learn to love you."

Emma was not so sure. A sense of dread still hovered inside her, and she couldn't manage to shake it away. "Let us face our challenges one at a time," Emma said through a deep breath. "First, how am I going to leave your study now without being caught?" She leaned close to him with an accusatory smile. "Did you think of that before pulling me through the doorway? Your mother could be lingering in the corridor as we speak."

"Perhaps I never want you to leave." He smiled, and she knew she would never grow tired of the sight of his face like that, his eyes flickering over every one of her features as if he were studying for an exam.

Emma pressed her lips together, the recent memory of their kissing at the forefront of her mind. "If I don't return to my room, my maid will be sure to gossip."

"Let her gossip about us for one night. Tomorrow she will have the elopement to gossip about." Harry leaned forward, capturing her lips with his. His kiss was deep and slow, passionate enough to make her head spin. He pulled back, a smile returning to his face. "Stay for an hour. By then, my mother will have surely stopped lurking in the corridor. After all, I have a deck of cards."

Emma took a moment to gather her composure. How could he kiss her like that and speak of cards seconds later? She laughed, a breathless sound. "Do you?"

"I also have a chess board." He gestured at the corner of the room.

Emma placed one hand on her hip. "I challenge you to a game of piquet."

He hurried to his desk, picking up his spectacles and placing them on his nose. "I accept your challenge."

She wanted to hate those spectacles, but she had always found them adorable beyond words. She burst into laughter, a sense of release accompanying it. They played their game of piquet, and she won just as easily as she had when they were younger. When the game was over, Harry walked her to the door, his eyes drooping with weariness and raw admiration at the same time. Seeing Harry like this was so new, yet so familiar at once. There was nothing standing between them, at least not there in the quiet, candlelit study. Outside, there were obstacles yet to be demolished, but the ones that had stood between them for years were gone. She didn't have to pretend she didn't like him. Being there with him felt like a delicious secret of some kind, and it was completely thrilling.

He pulled her into his arms, and she rested her head against his chest. "Do you know the way to your room in the dark?" Harry asked, his voice vibrating against her skin.

"Yes." She tilted her chin up to look at him. "I shall need my rest. We have an elopement to plan tomorrow."

"I wish it was our own."

Emma laughed. "It soon may be if your mother continues her attempts to interfere."

"Her attempts are in vain." Harry kissed Emma's forehead softly. "She won't have her way. I promise."

Emma believed him. All her fears and doubts seemed to lose themselves when he looked at her. His lips found hers again. She kissed him until she lost track of the ticking of the clock in the corner. The game of piquet had been enjoyable, but not as enjoyable as it was to kiss Harry—to trust that he would be hers forever. That belief was intoxicating, and she clung to it with everything she had. After planning to assist in an elopement that might ruin Miss Fitzroy's connection to her family, kissing Harry in the late hours of the night behind the closed door of his study felt like a small scandal in comparison.

After a few minutes, Harry pulled away with a groan, an unruly smile on his face. "I would keep you here forever if I could, but we have a facade to maintain a little longer."

"*You* were the one who refused to deny your feelings for me to your mother. The facade is crumbling as we speak."

Harry chuckled. "Let us hope it lasts one more day."

Emma could hardly wait to stop pretending, to stand up to Mrs. Coleman and to know that Miss Fitzroy and Mr. Hale were happy together.

One more day.

CHAPTER TWENTY-TWO

"The coach will be prepared by midnight." Emma stood near the window in Miss Fitzroy's room. Her trunk had been packed, tucked behind her bed. The sun had begun setting, leaving behind streaks of orange light between the clouds.

The day had felt like an eternity.

Every muscle in Emma's body had been tense, and her anxiousness had made it difficult to sit still during tea that afternoon, especially with Lady Burgess and Mrs. Coleman watching her so attentively. The two women had seemed more interested in Emma than in Miss Fitzroy, and their attention had been...unsettling. They had been acting so peculiar. Emma excused it with the observation that *everyone* in the household was on edge. The tension was tangible in every room and in every face.

Miss Fitzroy knew all the details of the plan for the elopement, and Harry had relayed the same to Mr. Hale. Everything was in order. All that was left to do was to make it through dinner without causing any suspicion. Emma and Mr. Hale had both thought it best to remain in their respective rooms for dinner in order to keep Mrs. Coleman and Lady Burgess as happy as possible throughout the evening. Harry and Miss Fitzroy could play the part of an engaged couple for one meal, and by the next day, the truth would be out.

"I cannot adequately express my gratitude to you, Miss Eastwood." Miss Fitzroy clung to Emma's hand, a gleam of excitement in her dark eyes. "I shall never forget your kindness."

"It is nothing," Emma said. "It brings me joy to see you and Mr. Hale so happy. I always wondered why he never smiled. Now I know that it was because he was without you."

"I thought the same about Harry." Miss Fitzroy gave a quiet laugh. "He was so business-like and stoic all the time. Much like I was."

"The business of love is *very* complicated," Emma said with a faint smile. "But I've learned that there is no worthier ambition, and there is nothing that brings greater profit."

Miss Fitzroy's smile grew, and she and Emma laughed together, her nerves subsiding for a brief moment.

"I shall remember that, Miss Eastwood."

After eating her meal in her room, Emma listened to the notes of the pianoforte floating up from the drawing room. The pianist was likely Miss Fitzroy, and the tune she played could not have been more fitting to the adventure she would embark on that evening. Emma and Harry had done all they could to arrange it, and now there was nothing more to do but watch from their windows as the carriage took Mr. Hale and Miss Fitzroy away. It would be impossible to sleep in anticipation of the next morning when their absence was discovered—as well as Miss Fitzroy's letter explaining where she had gone.

Emma rubbed her palms over her skirts, pacing her room until the music from the drawing room had long ended. There were still hours to pass before Miss Fitzroy and Mr. Hale would sneak away. How would she pass the time without losing her mind? She was nervous enough already.

A light tap sounded on the door, and then came Isabel's voice. "Miss?"

"Come in." Emma sat on the edge of her bed, hoping to appear calm and nonchalant.

The maid gave a curtsy as she entered, her fingers fidgeting with her apron. "I've come with a message for ye."

Emma tipped her head to one side, frowning. "What is it?"

"Master Coleman be lookin' for ye, miss. I've been sent to tell ye that he's out on the other side of the hill waiting for ye."

Emma's brow furrowed. At his hour? If he had arranged to meet her to discuss something, then it must have been important. But why all the way outside on the other side of the hill? "Very well, thank you," she muttered.

Her confusion swirled as Isabel took her swift leave of the room.

Emma hurried to put on her cloak, opting not to bring a candle on her walk out to the hillside. She managed to sneak away unnoticed. All the guests must have gone to bed. The chilled night air cut through her cloak easily, and soon she was shivering. The coastal wind never seamed to cease, whipping at her hair and numbing her fingers. Why hadn't she thought of putting on her gloves? Isabel's message had seemed too urgent. What could Harry have to say to her?

She walked over the crest of the hill, wrapping her blanket more tightly around herself. She squinted into the darkness. Had he not arrived yet? Where was he?

Just as she started the descent down to the base of the hill, a movement from her left made her jump in surprise. Two men—dressed in the Garsley livery—lunged toward her, taking her by either arm. She started to scream, but one of their gloved hands cupped over her mouth.

"We mean you no harm." The man's deep voice whispered near her ear.

Her heart raced, her muscles clenching with terror. How the devil did he expect her to believe him? She writhed under the grip of both men, but it was futile. They tugged her easily down the hill, her feet barely touching the ground. She tried to jerk her face free of the footman's hand, but he only held her tighter.

They didn't stop walking—and she didn't stop her struggle—until they reached the trees. A carriage waited in the darkness, two lanterns lighting the front of it. The restless horses shifted at the struggle of Emma's approach.

"We've had orders to send you to London," the man to her right said. "An apartment and lady's maid have been hired for your use."

Her mouth remained covered until they pushed her into the carriage, climbing inside with her and closing the door.

Emma shoved their arms away, pressing her back into the cushioned seat. "Are you mad? This is unlawful. Did Mrs. Coleman pay you to do this?" The question sprang to her lips without hesitation. There was no one else who would have done it.

The two men exchanged a glance. It was answer enough.

Emma lunged for the door, but the footmen were too quick. They blocked the way before she could reach it. "You're not leaving this carriage 'til we reach the inn. You'll stay a night there before we finish the journey tomorrow. We're told not to let you out of our sight until Mr. Coleman's wedding's taken place."

Emma gaped at them. "A wedding is not taking place! Mrs. Coleman doesn't know it yet, but the engagement has already been broken off."

"You may try all you like, miss, but we'd like to get paid."

Young, daft fools. The two footmen could not have been older than twenty. Didn't they realize they could be arrested for this? How would it appear when they were seen dragging a lady into an inn against her will? Did Mrs. Coleman think Emma would simply succumb to the idea and not put up a fight? Her anger raged, making her cheeks burn hot. Mrs. Coleman must have also paid Isabel to send her 'message' that evening. It had been a trap.

Emma exhaled through her nose in an attempt to calm her anger for the time being. She would not be able to escape yet, not with the two men standing guard over the door. She would have to be patient. If she pretended to accept her circumstances, then she had no doubt that the two bacon-brained footmen would loosen their guard. She had traveled far on foot before. She could make her way back to Garsley if she made her escape at their first stop. Her teeth gritted. She no longer had any desire for Mrs. Coleman's good opinion. She didn't want to be wanted or welcomed by her anymore.

Let Mrs. Coleman hate her. Emma was not particular fond of the woman either. In fact, she was now even more determined to marry Harry and make the woman miserable by doing so.

Any self-pity or sadness she had felt in regard to her future mother-in-law vanished, and strangely enough, her confidence soared. Mrs. Coleman would regret this as heartily as the two footmen would. If she thought this would solve anything, she was wrong. It would only drive Harry farther away. The footmen blinked at her, shoulders squared as they guarded the door.

Emma sat back, crossing her arms. Pretending to comply was the only idea she had. "Very well. If I am your captive, then let us be on our way."

CHAPTER TWENTY-THREE

Harry's mood was a stew of a thousand emotions the next morning. Relief, nervousness, and hope were the most prevailing.

The elopement had been a success.

He had watched the carriage containing Miss Fitzroy and Mr. Hale drive away after midnight. His and Emma's involvement, as far as he knew, was undetectable. That morning, Lady Burgess would be in receipt of her daughter's letter, and chaos would break loose at Garsley. *That* he wasn't looking forward to, but he could hardly wait to see Emma. She must have been feeling as nervous as he was.

He paused at his bedchamber door to calm his emotions. He needed to act as if nothing was amiss. Striding out into the corridor, he made his way to the breakfast room. Would Emma meet him there?

Without the slightest idea of what to expect behind the door, Harry walked cautiously inside. Mother sat at the table, hands crossed in front of her, spine straight as she watched the servants line the sideboard with food. The sunlight from the window glinted off her brown irises, making them gold and translucent. "Good morning, Harry."

"Good morning." He walked with slow steps. After their last argument, he hadn't expected such a warm greeting.

She gestured casually at the salver on the table. "There is a letter for you. The sender is not named."

Harry frowned, crossing the room and taking the letter from the salver. His name was scrawled across the front, but nothing more. He glanced at Mother and the intense interest on her face as he tore the seal.

Dear Harry,

I thank you for your hospitality these weeks, but I have found the courage to pursue my dream. I have departed for London, and there I will stay in order to begin my profession on the stages. I wish you all the best in your forthcoming marriage.

Sincerely,
Emma

Harry sucked in his cheeks, holding his breath for several seconds. He closed his eyes.

How daft did Mother believe him to be?

He crumpled the letter in one hand, lowering it to his side. "What is the meaning of this?"

Mother blinked up at him, her fallen expression wincing at his reaction. Was it not what she had expected? She raised her eyebrows, eyes round. "What does it say?"

"I think the author could best answer that question." Harry tossed the letter toward her, leaning over the table. "I would recognize Emma's hand. Besides that, you have entirely misrepresented her. She doesn't dream of singing in London. She dreams of a life with me, and *that* she shall have whether you like it or not."

Mother spluttered, shaking her head. "Your accusations are unfounded! Do you truly believe I forged that letter? Tell me what it says at once."

Harry exhaled, closing his eyes. "Where is she?"

"Perhaps she has finally decided to abandon her efforts to steal you from Miss Fitzroy. I commend her for her surrender."

Harry took a step closer, eyeing her dangerously. "Tell me what you have done."

Mother released a huffed breath. "Harry, you are being ridiculous. If Miss Eastwood is not here, then she must have left of her own accord."

Panic raced through his veins. He banished the prickle of doubt that followed her words. He knew Emma wouldn't leave. This wasn't right. "She wouldn't choose to leave. We are engaged."

Mother's eyes flew open wide. "You are *engaged* to Miss Fitzroy."

Harry shook his head. "My engagement to Miss Fitzroy has been broken for days now." He leaned over Mother's shocked expression. "I love Emma, and if you have done anything to hurt her, you will be living out the rest of your days with Richard." Harry's elder brother had inherited their small childhood home when their father died, and Mother had been eager to move away from it in favor of the grand castle. He had allowed her to stay, but that invitation had its limits.

"The hotel!" Her wild eyes filled with tears, her teeth gritting as she rose to her feet. "You would give up your dream for that wretched girl? Harry, I beg you to reconsider." She reached for his arm, but he pushed her hand away.

"Where is she?"

Mother's nose wrinkled, tears dripping down her cheeks. In an instant, she collapsed back into her chair, burying her face in her hands. Her body shook with sobs.

Harry's panic intensified.

"Mother." He gripped her shoulder, forcing her gaze back to his. "What have you done?"

She sniffed, taking a long moment to gather her words. Her raspy voice shook with sobs. "I knew you loved her. I couldn't bear the thought of losing the hotel. It has been all I've dreamed of since your father died. It is the one thing that can bring me hope and happiness." She filled her cheeks with air, releasing it slowly. "You shall never forgive me."

"*Where* is Emma?" Harry didn't care for Mother's dramatic excuses at the moment. She looked like a criminal —one who was acting remorseful in the hopes of being pardoned.

"She is on her way to London." She looked up from the table, her eyes bloodshot. "I...arranged her departure."

"Arranged?"

Mother twisted the ring on her finger. "I...well, I don't suspect she went willingly."

Harry cursed under his breath, turning toward the door. "In one of our coaches?"

"With two footmen."

Mother had seemed so concerned with Emma's propriety when she had first arrived at Garsley, and now she had sent her alone to London with two footmen as company? Desperation wrapped around him—to find her, to bring her home—until he could hardly think clearly.

"Please, Harry!" Mother's frantic voice drifted toward him. "Let her go. It is not too late to marry Miss Fitzroy."

He turned around, his anger boiling over. "It *is* too late. You have already lost." He tore the door open just as Lady Burgess approached the doorway, her face contorted with distress. Her grey-streaked hair was still tied in rags. In one hand, she held a letter.

Harry would leave Lady Burgess to the task of relaying the news to Mother.

He needed to find Emma.

Emma trudged through a puddle of mud, no longer caring about the state of her boots or hem. They were beyond saving. She wiped at the perspiration on her brow, squinting through the speckles of morning light that came through the leaves in the trees around the path. How many miles had they traveled before she had escaped? By her estimation, it had been at least ten miles before she and the footmen had stopped at the inn. She had entertained them with lies along the way about how excited she was to sing in London. At the inn, they hadn't even cared to guard her door, and surely they hadn't expected that a lady would embark on a ten mile journey on foot through the woods alone.

But what was ten when she had already done eighteen?

Fortunately, the path was clear, and she was fairly certain she was headed in the right direction. Her confidence waned a bit when she reached a fork in the road.

"Drat," she muttered, planting her hands on her hips as she considered each one. She had spent the first two hours of the walk thinking of how happy it would make her to see Mrs. Coleman's dismay when she walked through the doors of Garsley and announced her plans to marry Harry. There was no doubt Harry would dismiss all the servants who were involved in Mrs. Coleman's scheme. He might even dismiss his mother from her right to live at Garsley.

Nothing sounded sweeter at the moment. Not even a tall glass of water and a pile of sugared biscuits. Emma's stomach grumbled at the thought.

Far in the distance, the sound of hoofbeats struck the ground. She stepped behind a nearby tree, peeking out from behind it. If the person looked reputable, she might ask for directions. She likely had another three miles before she would reach Garsley. Her legs and back already ached from the first seven.

As the rider came into view, she jerked back in surprise, then waved her hands wildly. It was Harry. She gasped with disbelief, tears springing to her eyes.

Harry brought his horse to a halt and then dismounted in one swift motion, rushing toward her.

Despite her horrible night, the strange urge to laugh

overcame her, and soon she had dissolved into relieved giggles. She had hoped Harry would find her on her walk back, but she had been trying to keep her expectations at bay.

She threw her arms around him, and he held her tight for several seconds. He leaned back to look at her. His chestnut hair was wild from the wind, but she found that it suited him well. "Emma," he groaned, his eyes trailing all over her. "Are you hurt?"

"I've walked much farther before." She couldn't focus on anything besides how happy she was that Harry was there, standing in front of her, holding her as if he planned to never let go.

"My mother's behavior has been insufferable. She is a danger to you, and so she won't be permitted to stay at Garsley any longer. My brother and his wife will have to take her in to their dower house, and heaven help them."

Emma had never been more relieved. She would hope that eventually they might be reconciled, but at the moment, she required distance from the woman who had arranged to have her abducted. She gasped, remembering what she had missed from the night before. "Did Mr. Hale and Miss Fitzroy—"

"They are long gone." Harry smiled, brushing aside Emma's hair. "As a result, I'm afraid there is a riot taking place at Garsley as we speak."

Emma grimaced. "I'm glad to have drawn you away for a time."

"I'm not glad for the circumstances," Harry said, shaking his head with a bewildered smile. "How did you manage to escape?"

"It was not difficult. The footmen were easily fooled." Though the ordeal had been frightening, she had never felt that she was in danger. She had known she would make it back to Harry. Mrs. Coleman's attempts to keep them apart had been an inconvenience at worst.

Harry led her toward the horse by the hand. "Let us ride home and hope that the worst of the commotion has passed." He tossed a glance at her from over his shoulder. "You look remarkably well for having just walked for miles through the dirt."

Emma felt a hint of heat rise to her cheeks. She was still not accustomed to being complimented by Harry. His flirtatious smile was new as well, and she struggled to take it seriously.

"Do not lie to me, Harry George Coleman." She tugged her hand away and tried to stride past, but he caught her from behind. He spun her around to face him, a wide grin on his face.

"I hate when you call me that," he said amid a laugh.

"You ought to grow accustomed to it if you plan to marry me."

He gave an exasperated sigh.

"Does that give you cause to reconsider?"

He tugged her forward, pressing a soft kiss to her lips before shaking his head. "Never."

She stared up at him, taking hold of his lapels. "What are we to do when we return? I'm not certain I want to face Lady Burgess and your mother until the worst of their reaction has passed." She paused. "Might we hide in the keep?"

Harry chuckled. "I won't hide you away, nor my feelings and intentions any longer. You are the future mistress of

Garsley." To her surprise, his eyes filled with tears. He blinked fast. "You belong there. With me."

At the sight of his tears, her own came out of nowhere. Her smile was wide enough to make her cheeks ache. "I love you, Harry George Coleman."

He groaned, but pulled her in for another kiss anyway.

EPILOGUE

S IX MONTHS LATER

"We have a letter from Mrs. Hale," Emma said as she practically flew onto Harry's bed. He felt as if he were still half asleep, the early morning light spilling through the window. Emma bounced twice before falling beside him, her golden curls splaying out around the pillow.

He rubbed his eyes, laughing as she unfolded the parchment. "Where have you been? It's barely past dawn." The last time he had seen her, she had been sleeping peacefully beside him, but now her eyes were wild with excitement, a magenta spencer jacket buttoned all the way up to her neck.

"I went on a walk."

"Naturally." Harry grinned, rolling over to read the letter over her shoulder.

"Mr. Hale has sold his estate and they have purchased a house in the Cotswolds," Emma said as her eyes skimmed hungrily over the page. "Lady Burgess has visited them there. They are expecting a child." Emma sighed as she relayed what Harry could clearly read himself. "They are quite content."

Her relieved blue eyes met his, and Harry felt the same relief that was displayed on her face. He sat up on one elbow, a chill running across his bare shoulders and chest as the blanket fell away. Heating a large castle was difficult with winter approaching, but the expenses he had saved by not building his hotel had allowed him to have plenty of firewood and servants employed to help around the castle. The past six months had been the happiest of his life, and he was reminded of that fact each time he looked at Emma. His wife.

Mother had grudgingly attended their wedding before taking her journey to East Sussex to live with Harry's brother and his wife. She had understood that such consequences were mild compared to what she deserved for having Emma abducted and sent to London. She had even apologized, which had shocked both Harry and Emma. He had reason to hope that one day they might be reunited with less enmity.

"Do you take all the credit for the Hales' happiness?" Harry asked in a teasing voice as Emma continued to stare at the letter.

She pursed her lips. "Most of it."

"Well, you may take credit for all of mine."

She laughed, the sweetness of her smile completely

undoing him. He hooked one arm behind her, throwing off her balance enough to make her fall against him. She kissed the corner of his jaw, then his lips twice before hovering above him with a smile. "I shall happily claim the honor."

NEXT IN THE CASTLES & COURTSHIP SERIES

Next up in the multi-author Castles & Courtship series!
A Noble Inheritance by Kasey Stockton

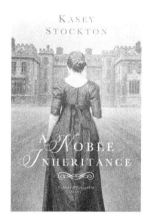

ALSO BY ASHTYN NEWBOLD

Noble Charades Series

Larkhall Letters Series

Brides of Brighton Series

Standalone novels
To Marry is Madness
In Pursuit of the Painter
The Last Eligible Bachelor
An Unwelcome Suitor
Her Silent Knight
Mischief and Manors
Lies and Letters
Road to Rosewood
Novellas & Anthologies
The Earl's Mistletoe Match
The Midnight Heiress
At First Sight

ABOUT THE AUTHOR

Ashtyn Newbold grew up with a love of stories. When she discovered Jane Austen books as a teen, she learned she was a sucker for romantic ones. Her first novel was published shortly after high school and she never looked back. When not indulging in sweet romantic comedies and regency period novels (and cookies), she writes romantic stories of her own. Ashtyn also dearly loves to laugh, bake, sing, and do anything that involves creativity and imagination.

Connect with Ashtyn Newbold on these platforms!
    INSTAGRAM: @ashtyn_newbold_author
    FACEBOOK: Author Ashtyn Newbold
    TIKTOK: @ashtynnewboldauthor
    ashtynnewbold.com

Printed in Great Britain
by Amazon